The Case of the Counterfeit Criminals

Frank moved over to the window of the sneaker factory outlet and looked out. The black four-by-four was still there, but the guys who were in it were gone.

From the other side of the room came the murmur of low voices. Frank crept closer and peered around the end of a rack of sneakers. He heard a guy talking to the stock boy say, "You said you could come across with the goods, Devin. And you haven't."

Suddenly Frank heard a shoe scrape behind him. He whirled around in time to see two guys with mean expressions come barreling toward him. Frank's martial-arts training took over. He lashed out his left foot, finding a target in his first assailant's stomach.

As soon as the second attacker came within reach, Frank grabbed the guy's outstretched arm and threw him over his shoulder. The attacker went flying into a rack of shelves, and sneakers came crashing down on him.

Suddenly something hard slammed into the back of Frank's head. He felt himself falling. He stretched out his hands to break the fall. Then Frank closed his eyes, and everything went black.

Hardy Boys
Mystery Stories

Available from MINSTREL Books

114

The
HARDY BOYS®

THE CASE OF THE COUNTERFEIT CRIMINALS

FRANKLIN W. DIXON

A
MINSTREL®
BOOK

PUBLISHED BY POCKET BOOKS

New York   London   Toronto   Sydney   Tokyo   Singapore

A MINSTREL PAPERBACK *ORIGINAL*

 A Minstrel Book published by
POCKET BOOKS, a division of Simon & Schuster Inc.
1230 Avenue of the Americas, New York, NY 10020

Copyright © 1992 by Simon & Schuster Inc.
Front cover illustration by Daniel Horne

Produced by Mega-Books of New York, Inc.

ISBN: 0-671-73061-4

First Minstrel Books printing June 1992

10 9 8 7 6 5 4 3 2

THE HARDY BOYS MYSTERY STORIES is a trademark of Simon & Schuster Inc.

THE HARDY BOYS, A MINSTREL BOOK, and colophon are registered trademarks of Simon & Schuster Inc.

Printed in the U.S.A.

Contents

THE CASE OF THE
COUNTERFEIT CRIMINALS

1 Track Meet Threats

"Wow, we really drew a crowd today, Frank!" Joe Hardy exclaimed, his blue eyes sparkling. "Look at all these cars!"

"This track meet's important," eighteen-year-old Frank replied. Joe's older brother slowed the van and turned into the Bayport High School parking lot. "Holman High has a top-notch team this year."

"Bayport's team isn't so bad, either," Joe said, grinning. He poked Frank lightly on the shoulder. "Especially with the dynamic duo of Frank and Joe Hardy filling out their team."

Frank parked, then twisted his lean, six-foot-one frame to grab his gym bag from the back. As they got out of the van, Frank noticed a black four-by-four pull into a space about twenty feet away. The

1

truck was hard to miss. The body sat high over fat off-the-road tires. The top was off, revealing a massive roll bar. The driver was a tall, lanky guy with close-cut blond hair. He looked tense. He also looked familiar, but Frank couldn't quite place him.

The driver and the three other guys in the four-by-four were all wearing maroon and gray Holman High jackets. They jumped out and started for the gym.

When they drew even with Frank and Joe three of them brushed past, but the driver deliberately elbowed Joe in the back.

"Hey, what is this?" Joe said, spinning around.

"You think you own the sidewalk?" the guy from Holman demanded.

"No, but I've got as much right to it as you do," Joe retorted.

One of the others, a dark-haired guy with broad shoulders, turned back and said, "Come on, Eric. Save your energy for the meet."

"Butt out, Lonnie," the blond guy replied. "I don't have to put up with anything from a bunch of wimpy Bayport kids."

Joe faced him with narrowed eyes. "Listen, pal," he said. "I don't know what your problem is, but maybe you should just mind your own business."

"I'll do what I want," Eric said. "If you don't like it, tough." He took a step toward Joe.

"Take it easy," Frank urged, moving to separate the two.

But right at that moment, Lonnie grabbed Eric's

arm, just above the elbow. "Come on, Eric. You know what Coach said," Lonnie muttered under his breath. "One more fight and he'll bounce you off the team, no matter how fast you can run. And if that happens, you can kiss that scholarship good-bye."

Eric's face turned pale as he jerked his arm away. "Okay, okay," he said sullenly. "I'll let it pass, this time." He gave Joe one last dirty look and then walked away.

"Sorry, guys," Lonnie said. "He's on kind of a short fuse. I'm Lonnie Jacobs, captain of the Holman High track team. No hard feelings?"

"No, that's okay," Frank replied. He introduced himself and Joe. They all shook hands. "By the way," Frank added, "what's his event?"

Lonnie gave him a surprised look. "You guys don't know?" he asked. "That's Eric Dresser, our best sprinter. At our last meet he almost tied the state record for the hundred meters."

"Oh, great," Joe groaned. "That's my event. You mean I'm going to be running against him? I just hope he's not in the next lane. He might try something sneaky."

Lonnie laughed. "Don't worry about it," he said. "Eric's a total champ when he's competing. The only thing you need to watch out for is that he comes off the starting blocks like a rocket. You Bayport guys will be eating his dust."

"We'll see about that," Joe replied in the same good-humored tone.

3

"Come on," Frank said. "Let's get changed and start warming up. We'll beat these Holman guys yet."

Near the front entrance of the gym, the Hardys spotted their friend Biff Hooper and stopped to talk. After a few minutes Joe went on ahead. Inside the boys' locker room, he paused. The Holman track team had been given the lockers on the far side of the central aisle. Joe noticed Eric Dresser right away.

Joe grabbed an empty locker on the near side, set his bag on the bench, and started unpacking his gear. When he pulled out his new Wombat track shoes, he looked them over with a frown. Their turquoise and red uppers gave them a lot of attitude. And they were supposed to include all the latest high-tech developments. They ought to, Joe thought. With what he had paid for them, he could have bought half a dozen pairs of ordinary sneakers.

Now he was starting to wonder if he had been taken for a ride. Would Hexacell innersoles, Acronytril liners, and helium-filled pneumatic springs really help him run a hundred meters any faster? He doubted it. Still, he had to admit that he liked using the built-in pump to adjust the fit around his heels and insteps.

As he unbuttoned his shirt, Joe glanced around. Fred Tolliver, another Bayport sprinter, was putting his stuff in a locker in the next aisle. Joe went over to him and talked tactics for a couple of minutes.

4

When he turned back, some of the guys from Holman High were standing in front of his locker.

Joe hurried over to see what was going on. He found Eric holding one of his new track shoes.

"Hey, what do you think you're doing?" Joe demanded. "Put that down!"

"Relax, Max," Eric replied. He slowly put the turquoise and red shoe down, then took a step backward. "We were just admiring the footwear."

One of the other guys gave Joe an uncomfortable look. "I saw an article about the new Wombats in this month's *Running* magazine," he said. "But this is the first time I've seen them up close and personal. Do you like them?"

"I haven't made up my mind yet," Joe admitted. "I just got them a couple of weeks ago."

"They look pretty rad," a third guy said. "I'm thinking about getting a pair myself. Who carries them around here?"

"I got mine at Benlow's, over at the Bayport Mall," Joe replied. "They've got a pretty decent selection."

From across the aisle someone called, "Hey, come on, you guys, get changed. Coach is going to wonder if we got lost on our way over here."

The athletes from Holman went back to their side of the locker room. Joe picked up his new shoe and studied it.

"What's the matter, Joe?" he heard Frank ask from behind his shoulder. "Do the colors clash with your shorts or something?"

Joe pretended to throw the shoe at his brother. Then he laughed and settled down to the business of changing into his track clothes.

Frank took his second try at the long jump, then stood up and dusted himself off. Pushing his dark hair off his face, he waited to hear the official measurement.

"Eighteen feet, four inches," the judge announced through the loudspeaker.

Frank pulled on his warm-up suit, feeling pleased with the results. It wasn't my best ever, he reflected, but it could put me in second place. Glancing at his watch, he realized it was almost time for the hundred-meter race, Joe's event.

As Frank crossed the field to the shadow of the grandstand, he paused to zip up his jacket. The sky was a brilliant blue, thanks to a cold front that had dropped down from Canada during the night. It was warm in the sunlight, but now that he was in the shade, he felt a chill in the air. It might be spring now, but winter wasn't that far behind.

Joe was sitting on the grass near the starting line, doing some stretches. He waved to Frank.

"How are you doing?" Joe asked when Frank squatted down next to him.

"Not bad," Frank replied. "I'm in good shape for second place. If Chuck Grade, Holman's best jumper, flubs his second try, I even have a shot at coming in first."

"Hey, way to go, bro!" Joe exclaimed. "I guess

the ball's in my court now. That guy Eric is going to be tough to beat.''

The announcer's voice said, "Entrants for the hundred-meter sprint, to the starting line, please. Hundred-meter sprint to the starting line."

"That's you, Joe," Frank said, gripping his brother's hand in a shake. "Go for it."

Joe stood up, took off his warm-up suit, and touched his toes a couple of times. "I'll see you a few seconds from now," he said with a grin.

While Joe jogged to the starting blocks, Frank headed down the track toward the finish line. Frank was still fifteen or twenty yards from the finish line when they heard the starter's pistol. He spun around and stood on tiptoe to see over the other spectators lining the track. The sprinters were in a tight pack, but it looked as if two of them were starting to pull ahead. One had short-cropped blond hair and looked like Eric. The other had blond hair, too, but cut longer. Then Frank recognized the six foot, muscular frame.

"It's Joe!" Frank cried out. "Come on, Joe!"

As they drew closer, Frank saw that his hunch was right. Eric and Joe were in the lead. They were running side by side, almost step for step with each other.

In the stands the crowd was on its feet, cheering loudly.

"Way to go, Joe!" Frank shouted, jumping up and down. "You can do it!"

Joe's face was a mask of pain. The veins in his

7

neck stood out like ropes. He picked up the pace in a last burst of effort, his arms and legs pumping madly. To Frank, it looked as though he was starting to inch ahead of the sprinter from Holman.

The two rivals drew level with Frank's position. No question about it, Joe was ahead. In a few more seconds he was going to take first place against one of the best sprinters in the state.

Frank was about to let out another shout of encouragement when he heard a loud pop. It sounded like a balloon bursting.

At that moment Joe suddenly broke stride. An instant later he tripped and tumbled to the ground.

2 Run-in at Benlow's

Frank quickly elbowed his way through the line of spectators and rushed to his brother's side. Joe was sitting up, rubbing his left ankle. His face was pale and drenched with sweat.

"Are you all right?" Frank demanded, kneeling down beside Joe. "What happened?"

Joe shook his head. "I don't know," he said. "I was running flat out, everything working just the way it should. And the next thing I knew, I was tripping over my own feet."

Joe untied his shoe and pulled it off, then felt his ankle with his fingertips. "It's not too bad," he reported. "Just twisted a little. I guess I didn't bring home any points this time," he added with a weak smile.

9

He started to get to his feet. At that moment, the Bayport coach came running over. He had a worried look on his face. "I saw what happened," he said with concern. "Don't move, Joe," the coach ordered. He knelt down and felt Joe's ankle, then gave a sigh of relief. "It's not broken, but you need to give it some rest for the next day or two. If it's not better by Monday, let's have Dr. Shelton take a look at it."

"Okay, Coach," Joe said. He picked up his shoe and started to pull it on. Suddenly he stopped and stared.

"So *that's* why I fell!" he exclaimed, holding up the shoe.

Frank took the sneaker from Joe and looked at it closely. He spotted a jagged tear, about an inch long, in the rubbery material along the side of the heel.

"You see what happened?" Joe asked. "I bet the pneumatic spring inside the heel burst. That's like driving a racing car and getting a blowout at top speed."

Frank studied the tear more closely. "I think you're right," he said. "But I've never heard of the air chamber blowing out in a running shoe. It must be defective."

"That's one possibility," Joe said grimly. "But I can think of another one. This morning in the locker room I caught Eric Dresser messing with my things. I bet he did something to my shoes."

10

The coach had been following their conversation. He gave Joe a worried look. "That's a pretty serious accusation," he said. "Unless you can back it up, I wouldn't go repeating it if I were you."

Joe gave a discouraged shrug. "All I know is that I had a chance to win the hundred meter. Thanks to my shoe, Eric won instead. And that could cost us the meet."

"Never mind that," the coach said, helping Joe to his feet. "You ran a good race, one of your best. That's what counts, not whether you were the first to break the tape. I'd better go check on the pole vault," he added. "And stay off that ankle, okay?"

Joe nodded and looked again at the ripped running shoe. Some of the sprinters from both schools had gathered around to see how Joe was. Joe showed them the damaged shoe and explained what had happened.

"That's funny," a guy from Holman said. "I know somebody who had the same thing happen to his new basketball shoes. I don't know if they were Wombats, though."

"I never had an air spring burst on me," Fred Tolliver said. "But last month the sole on one of my Wombat cross-training shoes came unglued at the front. They were just a couple of weeks old, too. I fixed it with rubber cement, but for the kind of money I paid for those shoes, they should have lasted longer than that."

"Hey, Hardy," a new voice said.

11

Frank looked around. Eric Dresser was standing behind him, a smug look on his face.

"Bad luck," Eric continued, shaking his head. "I guess you just couldn't go the distance, huh?"

Frank took a quick glance at Joe, but Joe kept his cool.

"Why don't we save the comments for later?" Joe said.

"Yeah," Fred Tolliver added, giving the Holman High runner a look of disapproval. "And maybe in the meantime you can get somebody to tell you about sportsmanship."

Eric glared at Fred, then at Joe and Frank. After a moment he turned and walked away.

"What *is* that guy's problem?" Fred demanded. "That chip on his shoulder must have come from a redwood!"

"I don't know," Joe said. "But whatever it is, I wish he'd stop trying to lay it on me." He bent down and pulled on the damaged shoe, then added, "I'll see you guys later. I'm going to go put on my old sneakers. They may not have all this high-tech stuff, but at least with them, I've never had a flat tire!"

Frank pushed through the crowd to the judges' table and checked the scoreboard. So far, Holman High was ahead, but not by much. The Holman coach must be biting his nails right down to the knuckles, Frank thought.

"Nice, even match," the guy standing next to

12

Frank said. Frank looked over and recognized Lonnie, the Holman High captain.

"It's pretty close," Frank said. "But you sound like you want it to be. I thought you Holman guys were into destroying the competition."

"I want to see my team win, sure," Lonnie said with a shrug. "But everyone turns in better performances when they're up against real competition. Hey, what happened to your brother in the hundred meter? I was sure he was going to upset Eric."

Frank weighed his words. He didn't want Lonnie to know of Joe's accusations about Eric. "What happened was that he fell when the air cell broke in his new Wombat running shoe," he said evenly. "It must have been defective."

"That's too bad," Lonnie said, shaking his head. "You know, at a meet a couple of weeks ago, a hurdler from Monroe had trouble with his new Wombats, too. The stitching came out all along the instep. For such expensive shoes, they don't hold up very well." He paused. "Well, catch you later. My event's up next." Lonnie took off.

Eager to find out who would win, Frank stayed by the judges' table until the meet was over. Holman High won, but by just a handful of points. Frank found Joe by the sprinters' lanes, and he and his brother made their way out of the stadium. On the way to the parking lot Joe couldn't stop talking about the race.

"If only I hadn't fallen," he said for what Frank was sure was the tenth time. "I think I could have

13

beat him. Even if I'd taken second place, or even third, we would have won the meet. I'm *sure* that guy Eric did something to my shoe. Why else would it pop like that?"

"Bad workmanship," Frank replied. He fished the keys from his pocket and unlocked the van. "Your shoe was defective, Joe. It's as plain and simple as that.

"Anyway," Frank went on. "Why would Eric want to sabotage your shoes? I mean, you're a good sprinter and all, but let's face it, you don't have a statewide reputation. He couldn't have known that you'd be his main competition."

"Logic," Joe grumbled. "That's all I ever get from you is logic. How about this? He just didn't like me. You saw how he went after me even before the race started."

Frank started the van and pulled out of the parking lot. "Maybe," he said. He waited for the traffic to move and turned to face Joe. "From what everybody was saying, you aren't the only one to have problems with a new pair of Wombats. I doubt if Eric is going around wrecking everybody's shoes."

"Maybe not," Joe conceded, "but explain this one. Why was Eric the only one who wasn't there for the closing ceremonies? Would *you* miss picking up your gold medal? Even if you knew it wasn't really gold? Even if you'd had to sabotage one of the other runners to win it?"

14

With a shrug Frank said, "Just because he cut out early doesn't make him guilty, Joe." Frank made a turn and said under his breath, "I just wish I could remember where I've seen him before. It's going to bug me for the rest of the weekend."

"Probably at another track meet," Joe said. "Hey. We're right near the mall. Do you mind stopping? Maybe my Wombats are defective. If so, I want to find out what Benlow's is going to do about it."

The mall was jammed with Saturday afternoon shoppers. Frank parked the van as close in as he could, then he and Joe hiked to the entrance. When they reached Benlow's Sporting Goods, they made their way to the back of the store through aisles of bowling balls, camp stoves, and high-fashion tennis wear in dazzling colors. Along the back wall were rows of athletic shoes in all the latest styles.

For some reason a group of people had gathered around a nervous-looking guy wearing a Benlow's blazer. The people were all shouting at him and pointing to the shoes in their hands.

"I spent a fortune for these," Frank heard a girl in white shorts and a purple tank top say. She was holding up a pair of walking shoes in purple and bright pink. "They came apart the third time I wore them!"

"And what about my basketball shoes?" a tall, skinny guy demanded. "The air pump broke the first time I used it."

15

A kid in khakis and a white knit shirt thrust a pair of black referee shoes under the man's nose. "Look at these," he said. "I just bought them last Wednesday, and already the stitching on the toes is coming out. We want our money back."

"Yeah! That's right!" the others in the group exclaimed. "Give us our money back!"

Frank turned to Joe and said softly, "What would you like to bet that they all bought Wombats in the last few weeks?"

"No bet," Joe replied. "You're definitely right."

The sales clerk took a step backward. "I'm sorry," he said. "I can't help you. I'm not authorized to give refunds. You'll have to come back during the week, when the store manager is here, and speak to him."

"I don't think that's going to make these people very happy," Joe said in a low voice.

A beefy teenager stepped forward. From the size of him, he looked as if he spent all his spare time pumping iron.

"That's not good enough," he said. He poked the clerk in the chest with his forefinger. "You people didn't have any problem with taking my money on a Saturday. So why can't you give it back on a Saturday?"

"I tell you, I don't have the authority," the clerk began to repeat. Then he broke off and called out, "Mr. Benlow? Mr. Benlow! We have a problem over here."

16

Frank looked around. The man the clerk called to was about six-feet-two, with broad shoulders, a thick neck, and a big pot belly.

"What's this?" Robert Benlow growled. "What's all the commotion?"

Everybody started talking at once. But in the middle of all the noise, Frank was able to make out the word *Wombat*. He shot Joe a glance. "See? What did I tell you!"

Benlow held his arms up over his head, like a referee signaling a touchdown. "Okay, okay," he said loudly. An uneasy silence fell. "Listen," he continued. "Wombat athletic shoes have the best unconditional guarantee in the business—against defects, poor workmanship, you name it."

"Great, I want my money back," the kid with the black eyebrows said.

"But," Benlow continued, ignoring him, "it's the company that guarantees them, not me. Any gripe you've got, take it up with the company, not here. Their offices are in Holman Heights, just twenty miles away. The address is on the shoe box."

"That's not good enough," the girl in the tank top insisted. "I bought these shoes here, not in Holman Heights."

"Yeah, right," others in the crowd growled.

Joe glanced over at Frank. "How long before somebody starts throwing things?" he muttered.

Frank shrugged. "Thirty seconds?" he suggested.

Benlow was apparently thinking along the same

17

lines. He plowed through the little crowd to an intercom mounted on the wall and pressed the button.

"Drop whatever you're doing," he said into the mike. "I need you out here, right now."

A garbled squawk answered him. A moment later the stockroom door swung open. Someone rushed out carrying a stack of shoe boxes that blocked his vision. He collided with Benlow, and the boxes tumbled to the floor.

Joe grabbed Frank's arm and pulled him behind a nearby mannequin. "Get down," he whispered urgently. "I don't want him to see us."

"Why not?" Frank asked, confused.

Joe pointed in the direction of the stock boy.

"It's him," he said. "It's Eric Dresser!"

3 The Wombat Connection

Frank ducked behind a rack of jogging suits and pulled Joe after him. "I don't think he saw us," he said in a low voice. "I told you I'd seen him somewhere before."

"It sounds as if Eric's got other things to worry about than us," Joe replied.

From the shoe department came the voice of the store owner. "Of all the stupid moves," he was saying. "Pick up those shoes and rebox them, right away. And make sure you get them all in the right boxes. We don't want any more foul-ups."

"But, Mr. Benlow," Eric said, "you told me I could leave at six. That's five minutes from now."

"You can leave when you're done," Benlow said, "and not a minute before. I let you take most of the day off, didn't I? So get back to work."

After Eric left, Benlow went back to talking to the customers with defective shoes. He explained how they could get their shoes replaced.

"I'm beginning to feel sorry for Eric," Frank whispered. "Come on, let's get out of here."

"What about my Wombats?" Joe protested. "I want to file a complaint."

"You heard what the man said—file it with the company, not with him."

Frank led the way to the parking lot. He and Joe got into the van, and Frank drove slowly through the lanes of parked cars.

"Let me guess," Joe said. "We're looking for a black four-by-four, right? The one Eric was driving this morning."

Frank nodded. "Uh-huh. And I think I see it, too, over there near the loading dock." He pulled into a vacant space and shut off the engine. The black roll bar of the four-by-four stuck up over the roofs of the other cars around it.

"I guess you've decided I was right about Eric after all," Joe remarked.

"You mean that he sabotaged your shoe because he wanted to boost his chances of beating you in the sprint?" Frank replied. "No way. If anything, it seems even more unlikely than before. What about those people in the store just now? Their Wombats had problems, too."

20

"Well, if you think he doesn't have anything to do with the defective Wombats, why are we sitting here watching his car?" Joe wanted to know.

Frank thought for a moment. "I don't like coincidences, that's all," he said. "Benlow's sells a lot of Wombats. A lot of them have problems, and Eric works there. That doesn't prove that he's causing the problems with the shoes, but it does make me want to take a closer look at him."

"Well, go ahead," Joe said. "There he is."

Frank looked up. The tall, lanky sprinter had just jumped down from the loading dock and was walking toward his car. Even from a distance his expression looked angry.

Frank started the van's engine. Just then Eric grabbed the roll bar of the four-by-four and vaulted into the driver's seat without bothering to open the door. An instant later, tires smoking, he roared off toward the exit.

"Where's he going in such a hurry?" Frank asked, hot on Eric's trail.

At the exit Eric didn't even slow down for the stop sign. He darted in front of a small foreign sedan. When the driver leaned on his horn, Eric paid no attention. He pulled into the opposite lane to pass the cars in front of him.

"He's a maniac," Joe declared, holding on while Frank took a sharp turn out of the parking lot.

Frank didn't answer. He was using all his driving skills to follow the four-by-four without taking too many risks.

"He just turned left onto Montgomery," Joe reported. "That's a shortcut to Holman Heights."

Frank paused to let a tank truck go by, then made his turn. He let out an exclamation and lifted his foot off the gas. The four-by-four was nowhere in sight.

"He couldn't have spotted us," Joe said. "He must have turned off onto a side street."

They cruised up and down Montgomery Street, peering down each side street for some sign of Eric's four-by-four. But the truck had disappeared. Finally Frank said, "Enough. He was probably just heading home, anyway."

Joe took one last look up Montgomery and checked his watch. "Well, since we've lost him, we should get home, too. It's almost time for dinner."

That night during dinner Joe and Frank told their parents and their aunt Gertrude, who lived with the Hardys, about the track meet. When Joe described his exploding athletic shoe, Gertrude was horrified.

"That's terrible!" she exclaimed. "You could have been badly hurt. Is your ankle all right?"

"It's fine," Joe assured her. "I just have to forget about running for a while."

"There's something very strange about this," Fenton Hardy said, frowning. "A company like Wombat is usually very careful about quality control. They have to be, to keep their reputation and stay in business. Now and then one or two defective products might slip through, but what you're describing sounds like more than bad quality control."

"That's what we're starting to think, too, Dad," Frank said. His father had been a leading member of the New York City Police Department before he retired and started his own detective agency. If Fenton Hardy thought something suspicious was up, Frank and Joe knew they had a real mystery on their hands.

"That many defective shoes can't be an accident," Frank said thoughtfully. "But what if one of Wombat's rivals has put somebody into their factory or bribed the quality inspector? By the time the company figures out what's happening, they could be down the tubes."

Joe snapped his fingers. "I've got another theory," he announced. "Frank, you remember when Billy Brown came back from a vacation in Mexico with that expensive Swiss watch? When it stopped working and he tried to get it fixed, he found out it was a counterfeit. But even the jeweler was fooled at first."

He paused and looked around the table. "Maybe the reason my Wombats turned out to be defective is that they aren't Wombats at all. Maybe they're badly made imitations."

"They're not *that* badly made," Frank pointed out. "They look exactly like real Wombats."

"Of course they do," Joe replied. "And a counterfeit twenty-dollar bill looks just like a real one. That's the whole idea."

23

Frank rubbed his chin thoughtfully. "Good point," he said. "But you can usually spot the fake if you know what to look for. After dinner we should take a closer look at those shoes of yours. We can compare them with my Wombat basketball shoes. I'm sure they're genuine."

In the cellar of the Hardy house was a small but up-to-date crime lab. After dinner Joe and Frank took the two pairs of athletic shoes down and started examining them.

"I don't see a thing," Joe said. "Either my shoes are real Wombats that are defective, or they're perfect imitations. I'm leaning toward my first idea again, that Eric sabotaged them."

Frank shook his head. "If it were just your shoes that had a problem, I'd go along with you," he said. "Let's run a couple more tests."

"I'll get out the ultraviolet lamp," Joe volunteered. "I bet these shoes look really wild under UV."

Joe plugged in the black light lamp and turned out the ceiling fixture. "Wow!" he exclaimed. The ultraviolet light made the turquoise parts of Joe's running shoe disappear completely, leaving only a brilliant red pattern that looked like flames. Frank's basketball shoe glowed white all over, except for the Y-shaped support bands along the sides.

"Different shoes, different glows," Joe said. "But I don't see how that helps us."

"Nope, I guess not," Frank agreed. "You might as well turn on the room lights." He took one last look at the shoe and noticed a mark that caught his attention.

"Look at this," Frank said to Joe. "There's something printed inside my shoe."

Joe picked up a magnifying glass. "It says, 'Passed, Number 32,' and a date from early last year. It must have been put there by the quality control inspector. Pass me my shoe."

Frank passed it over, then leaned close to look over Joe's shoulder. There was no sign of any printing inside the defective shoe.

"Maybe it was stamped inside the other shoe," Joe suggested. "I'll get it."

But there was no stamp inside the mate to the defective shoe, either.

Joe looked over at Frank. "We were looking for an important difference," he said. "And I think we just found one."

"You're right," Frank said. "But let's not jump to conclusions. My shoes are over a year old. Maybe they changed their procedures since then. Or maybe your shoes just happened to miss getting stamped."

"And just happened to be defective, too?" Joe replied. "That's a pretty big coincidence."

Frank nodded. "I know. But we still aren't sure if your Wombats are real or fake. We have to nail that down before we do anything else."

Joe sighed impatiently. "So how do we do that?" he asked.

"We should get in touch with somebody at the

Wombat Corporation," Frank continued. "It means waiting until Monday morning, but I don't see any way around it. They can tell us for sure if your shoes are counterfeit. And their cooperation will be a big help in solving the case."

On Monday morning Joe and Frank drove to the Wombat Corporation headquarters. It was in an office park in Holman Heights, about twenty miles from Bayport. The three-story building looked like a solid block of dark green glass. The Hardys found the main entrance and went inside. At the front desk was a guy who appeared to be just out of college, with horn-rim glasses and slicked-back hair.

"May I help you?" he asked.

"We'd like to speak to the person in charge of customer relations," Frank replied.

The man looked them over carefully. "This is in reference to . . . ?"

"A problem your company is having," Joe said. "A pretty serious problem."

"We can explain to the person in charge of customer relations," Frank added.

The receptionist studied Joe and Frank for another moment, then picked up his phone and spoke in an undertone.

"Please take a seat," he said, hanging up. "Someone will be with you shortly."

After about ten minutes the inner door opened

26

and a woman of about thirty, with shoulder-length dark hair, came toward them.

"I'm Karla Newhouse," she said, offering her hand. "I'm in charge of customer relations. What seems to be the problem?"

Frank introduced himself and Joe, then told her what had happened to Joe during the hundred-meter sprint. Joe pulled out the ruined shoe and handed it to her.

Turning it in her hands, Ms. Newhouse said, "At Wombat we're proud of our reputation for quality and reliability. I find it hard to believe that something like this could happen with one of our newest and finest models."

"I'm sure that's true," Joe said. "But that's some solid evidence you're holding."

"From what we've heard," Frank added, "Wombat's reputation is in a lot of trouble. We know about other customers who've bought defective shoes from your company. We may be able to help you, but we're going to need some cooperation."

"I see," Ms. Newhouse replied. Her face hardened. "Maybe we should continue this conversation in my office."

She led them through the inner door and along a corridor to an office with a desk, several chairs, and a computer terminal. On the walls were big color photos of different models of Wombats.

"Please sit down," she added. "I'll be back in a moment."

27

When Newhouse returned, she was accompanied by a heavyset, balding man with deep worry lines in his forehead. He was holding Joe's shoe.

"I understand you fellows think we have a problem with defective shoes," he said.

"That's right," Joe replied.

"And you're offering to help us with it, provided we cooperate with you. Is that right?"

Frank nodded.

"How much cooperation did you have in mind?" the man growled. "Five thousand dollars? Fifty thousand? And what made you imagine that we'd sit still while you tried to rip us off?"

"Now, wait a minute," Frank began.

"No, *you* wait a minute," the man replied. "Because that's exactly how long you've got before I call the police and have you both arrested for attempted extortion!"

4 The Facts About the Fakes

"Extortion!" Joe cried. "That's ridiculous."

"Karla," the man said, "would you mind calling security? Tell them we've got a couple of trouble-makers back here."

"We're not troublemakers," Joe said, spreading out his arms in frustration. "We're detectives, and we want to help your company."

Out of the corner of his eye, Joe saw Karla hesitate, her hand on the telephone.

"That's right," Frank added emphatically. "Please, before you make that call, answer one question for us. Is that defective shoe you're hold-ing really a Wombat, or is it a fake?"

The man blinked in surprise. He looked down at

the shoe and made a face. "What makes you think this shoe is a fake?"

"Just take a look. Please," Joe urged.

Frank and Joe stood by as the man held up the shoe and took a long look. After a bit of hesitation he raised an eyebrow and said, "Well, well, well. Maybe you kids *are* detectives."

"Then it *is* a fake," Joe said.

"I can't say for sure, not without running some tests on it. But if it's like the others we've been seeing the last few weeks, it's a fake, all right. How did you guess?"

"We checked it under ultraviolet light," Joe explained. "It doesn't have a quality control stamp like the one we found on my brother's pair of Wombats."

"We'd better sit down and discuss this," the man said, taking a seat and pointing to two other chairs. "Have a seat," he told Frank and Joe. "You, too, Karla. You should be in on this."

Ms. Newhouse didn't look thrilled at the idea, but she sat down, too.

"I'm Winston Brinkstead," the man continued. "Wombat's vice president of national sales. And you've already met Karla Newhouse, our new VP for customer relations."

Frank quickly introduced himself and Joe. "We've had a lot of experience as detectives."

Winston Brinkstead looked impressed. "Well, you kids are good enough to spot a fake Wombat, and that's good enough for me. I'm sorry about our misunderstanding a few minutes ago. When Karla told me that two teenagers were threatening to make trouble for the company unless we 'cooperated,' naturally I thought—"

"It's mostly my fault," Joe interrupted politely. "I should have done a better job of explaining what I meant."

"Mr. Brinkstead," Frank said. "Just now you seemed to be saying that Wombat's problem with the shoes is something pretty recent."

The man pressed his fingertips together and gazed across the room toward a poster for the Wombat Helio-Spring aerobic shoe.

"We've always had imitators," he began. "Small factories overseas that make quick, cheap copies with the look of our shoes, but without the special features and quality materials. They usually turn up at street fairs and cheap discount stores. Frankly, we don't pay much attention to them. No customer really thinks he's getting a real shoe for one-tenth the price."

"That wasn't what happened to me," Joe said. "I paid full price for those shoes, at an authorized Wombat dealer."

"That's one thing that's very different about these fakes," Brinkstead replied. "They're turning up at our regular dealers' stores."

"How long have you been aware of the problem, and how widespread is it?" Frank asked.

"That's very sensitive information, Winston," Karla put in. "I don't know that we ought to—"

31

"I'll take the responsibility," Winston replied. "I know this is really your department's ball, but it's time somebody tried to field it."

He looked back at Joe and Frank. "You understand that this is in confidence? These shoes started turning up about two months ago, mostly here on the East Coast. At first even we didn't spot them as fakes. All we knew was that customer complaints about defective shoes were increasing. Even when we realized what our problem was, no one was sure how to deal with it."

"Why not alert your customers?" Joe asked. "That way, the defective shoes won't hurt your company's reputation."

Winston nodded. "We thought of that. But a new group took over the management of the company at the beginning of the year. They're terrific people, with some wonderful ideas—"

"Why, thank you, Winston," Karla said, raising an eyebrow.

He continued as if he hadn't heard. "But they don't want to do anything that might hurt our relations with our dealers. We haven't even told our dealers about the counterfeit shoes."

Joe remembered the scene at Benlow's on Saturday afternoon. "Are you afraid that if they know, some of them will stop carrying Wombats?"

"Exactly," Winston replied. "If that happens in enough stores, we're dead. All the advertising in the world won't sell our shoes if a customer can't find them in a local store."

"What have you done to track down the source of the fakes?" Frank asked. "Or to find out how they are getting into the stores?"

"Practically nothing," Winston admitted. "Anything we do as a company might just call attention to the problem. Frankly, that's why I'm telling you boys all this. You don't have any official link to the company. You can nose around without attracting attention. And who knows? You may even come up with something."

"Thanks," Frank said eagerly.

Joe gave his brother a quick glance. Mr. Brinkstead's comment didn't sound like a vote of confidence to him.

"We'll need some help from you," Frank continued. "Can you give us Wombat dealers in this area and indicate which ones have sold the counterfeit shoes?"

Winston looked at him warily. "We don't want any publicity," he said. "What if a dealer wants to know why you're asking questions?"

"We can say that the company agreed to let us do a survey as a school project," Frank replied. "You can give us a letter, making it clear that we're not working for the company."

Winston thought for a few moments, then nodded agreement. "That should be all right," he said. "Karla, will you draw up that list of dealers for the boys? I'll draft a letter explaining what they're up to and asking store managers to cooperate with them."

With that, Brinkstead got up, shook hands with

Frank and Joe, and wished them luck. Within a few minutes Karla had given them a list of local Wombat dealers.

Frank and Joe spent the rest of the day going from one sporting goods store to another. At each one they showed the manager their letter from Brinkstead, then asked their "survey" questions about customer satisfaction, brand loyalty, and handling of defective merchandise.

"Another big zip," Joe said as they left a store called RE: Sport, on the main street of a town not far from Bayport. "We're wasting our time."

"I wouldn't say that," Frank replied. "We've learned one very important fact. Didn't you notice that the stores where the manager was cooperative hadn't had any problems with defective Wombats?"

Joe's eyes widened. "Hey, you're right," he said. "And the places where the manager was super-cagey with us were the ones that Karla marked as having sold most of the counterfeits."

Frank chewed on his pencil for a few moments before saying, "I see two possibilities. One, those managers were nervous because they knew they had a problem but didn't know what was causing it."

"Or, two," Joe said, "they were nervous because they had something to hide. In other words, they ordered the fake Wombats themselves. I vote for number two."

Frank said, "Put me down as undecided, leaning

toward number two. Maybe our next candidate will help swing my vote. Who is it?"

Joe checked the list. "Well, well," he said. "It's our old friend Robert Benlow, at the Bayport Mall. I wonder if we'll run into Eric."

"I hope not," Frank said. "I'd like to keep this investigation a secret as long as possible. I'm willing to bet Eric has heard about our reputation as detectives. If he finds out we've been asking questions, he'll add two and two."

"And get five," Joe joked. "Still, I see your point. By the way, according to Karla's list, Benlow's has sold more of the counterfeits than any other store in the area. I wonder if the fact that Eric works there has anything to do with that."

"Put that on our list of things to find out," Frank said as he started across the parking lot toward the van.

When they got to the Bayport Mall and entered the sporting goods store, Frank spotted Mr. Benlow near the wall of tennis rackets. He and Joe went over, introduced themselves, and showed him the letter from the Wombat Corporation.

The store owner obviously didn't recognize them from Saturday afternoon. He read the letter over twice and asked, "What's this project of yours?"

"It's for our marketing course," Joe explained. "We're doing a paper on the distribution of athletic shoes. You carry a lot of different brands, don't you?"

35

Mr. Benlow shook his head. "Only the four top ones," he said. "We can't stock all the different models each company puts out, only the ones that are most in demand."

"If the demand for a particular model falls off," Frank said, "you'd stop carrying it?"

"Sure," Mr. Benlow agreed. "That's good business. We can't carry shoes that don't sell."

"What about the brands you carry now?" Joe asked. "Are there any you're thinking of dropping from your stock?"

Mr. Benlow looked at them suspiciously, but Frank started taking notes to convince him they were really doing a report.

"All my shoes are selling well, and my customers are satisfied with what I carry," Benlow said finally. "Now, listen, boys, I'm pretty busy. Unless you've got—"

"Just a couple of quick questions," Frank interrupted. "You know, in school, you don't get a sense of how things really work. Let's say I work for you, as a buyer, the person who chooses what shoes you should stock. I study the catalogs and decide what to order this season. What then? Do I call the manufacturer?"

Mr. Benlow shrugged. "You might, I guess. More likely, the company salesman will call you and tell you what he thinks you ought to order."

"Then what happens?" Joe continued while Frank took notes. "Is the order delivered by the company, or by a trucking company, or what?"

36

"You're right," Benlow said with a hearty laugh. "You boys sure don't learn much in school. An independent delivery service brings the order over, usually a couple of days later. Our stock clerk checks the shipment and matches it with the order. We send the company a check for the shoes and cross our fingers that somebody buys them."

A saleswoman came over to tell Mr. Benlow that he had a phone call. The owner excused himself, and Frank and Joe left the store.

When Frank and Joe returned to the van, it was getting dark. "It's too late to check out any more stores before dinnertime," Frank said, starting up the van. "Let's head home and go over what we know."

On the way back to the Hardys, Joe said, "Benlow seemed pretty nervous when we asked him if any of his shoes weren't selling well."

"He still gave us a lot of useful information," Frank replied. "Now we know that there are three important steps in getting those counterfeit shoes into the hands—I mean, onto the feet—of customers. Somebody in the store has to order them, somebody has to deliver them, and the money for them has to get back to the counterfeiters somehow."

"You left out the most important step," Joe said, as they turned into their driveway. "Somebody, somewhere, has to *make* the counterfeits."

Frank parked in front of the garage, and they got out. As they climbed the steps to the back door,

Frank thought he heard a rustling in the bushes at the side of the house. He turned to look but didn't see anyone.

Then, suddenly, out of the darkness, Frank spotted a white ball come flying at top speed. It was headed straight for Joe!

5 Fancy Legwork

"Look out!" Joe heard Frank shout.

Instinctively Joe ducked. He felt something brush past his ear and smash into the doorjamb. Joe stared at the scarred doorframe for a second, then whirled around. From the other side of the bushes that lined the driveway came the sound of someone running.

"There he goes!" Joe shouted. "I'll get him!"

He vaulted over the railing of the porch and sprinted down the driveway. He had to favor his injured left ankle and became frustrated when he realized how much it slowed him down. As Joe reached the street, he heard the sudden roar of an engine. He jumped back as a car came roaring past him and disappeared around the corner of the block.

Joe shook his head in frustration and then headed back up to the house. "He got away," he told Frank. "I couldn't see who it was."

"Luckily he left us a souvenir," Frank replied. He held up a battered-looking baseball.

Joe reached for it, then pulled back his hand. "Any chance of lifting prints off it?" he asked.

"Not much," Frank said. "But we can try. It has a message on it, by the way. It says, 'Back off, or you'll be out of the game for good.'"

Joe snorted. "Not very original, but I get the message. If Eric can pitch that well, he should go out for baseball instead of track."

"Why Eric?" Frank demanded. "I thought you didn't get a good enough look to recognize the person."

Joe shook his head. "Well, I didn't. But he made it from here to the street awfully fast. Fast enough to be a champion sprinter. And from the glimpse I got of the car he escaped in, it could have been that four-by-four of his."

"That's pretty weak evidence," Frank said.

"I know," Joe admitted. "But how about this? Whoever sent us that warning did it because he knows we're on his case. Eric might have spotted us talking to Benlow this afternoon. If he found out we were asking questions about defective athletic shoes, he might have guessed what we're up to. And remember, he's in the best position to sneak the counterfeits into the store."

Frank thought for a moment, then said, "Well, maybe."

Joe grinned to himself. He knew Frank was sometimes a little unwilling to admit that anybody else could come up with good deductions.

"Let's get this baseball down to the lab and see if we can pick up any prints," Frank said.

In the lab Frank set the baseball on a fresh sheet of white paper. "What we've got here," he said, "is a Wickford brand baseball, the Ted Goring model. The hide cover is dirty and scarred. The message is printed in block letters, with what looks like a black felt-tip pen."

He turned to Joe. "Did I miss anything so far?" he asked.

Joe leaned closer, then reached for a magnifying glass. "I see some reddish orange particles caught in the stitching of the seams," he said. He took a fine-pointed knife and carefully scraped some of the particles into a clear plastic pill bottle. After capping and labeling the bottle, he added, "Looks like clay to me. Are there any red clay baseball diamonds around here?"

"I never noticed," Frank said. "But we can keep our eyes open. Hand me the powder sprayer and brush. Let's see if we can raise some prints."

A few minutes later Frank straightened up and said, "Well, we know two more things about our guy. He grips a baseball with his index and middle finger on one side and his thumb on the other. That

41

sounds like a trained pitcher. And he's smart enough to wear gloves when he's up to no good."

"Some help that is," Joe grumbled. "We already knew he was a good pitcher, by the way he threw the ball. And anybody over the age of five has heard of fingerprints." He stretched and stifled a yawn. "Let's put this stuff away and call it a night. Maybe we can pick up his trail tomorrow."

The next morning, after breakfast, Frank and Joe went over their list of stores that had sold the counterfeit Wombats. The next place to check was the Wombat factory outlet, in Holman Heights.

The outlet turned out to be a nondescript, low metal building in an industrial park adjacent to the office park where the headquarters building was located. Only a small sign next to the parking lot entrance, and another by the door, identified the building as the Wombat outlet.

"They don't seem very eager to let people know where the place is," Joe remarked as he parked near the door.

"It's probably a matter of keeping their dealers happy," Frank replied. "If customers knew they could buy their Wombats for less here, why would they pay full price at stores?"

They went inside. The salesroom was small, with tall metal racks of shoes, sorted by size. A young woman with short blond hair and a welcoming smile was standing behind the counter. "Hi," she said. "Can I help you with anything?"

"Could we speak to the manager?" Joe asked.

"That's me," the young woman replied. "I'm Marjorie Chaney."

Frank introduced himself and Joe, then gave her the letter from Winston Brinkstead. After reading it, she asked, "How can I help you guys?"

"First of all," Joe said, "we were wondering what was the point of a factory outlet. Is this where Wombat sends its mistakes?"

Marjorie Chaney shook her head and gave Joe a friendly smile. "No. In the back of the store we do have a rack of seconds that didn't pass the quality inspection because of some minor flaw. But most of what you see are first quality," she replied.

"Then why sell them for less?" Frank asked.

"Two reasons," she answered. "Some of these are discontinued models. Let's say, last fall our top of the line cross-training shoe was gray with purple accents. This spring the designers decided to change the accents to salmon. The leftover gray and purple models are sent over here."

"I get it," Joe said. "And what's the second reason?"

"The people at the factory never know for sure, in advance, how many pairs of a particular model will be ordered," Marjorie replied. "It's usually better to have too many than too few. Otherwise, you can't fill orders that come in."

She broke off her explanation to say, "Yes, Devin? What is it?"

43

A thin, black-haired boy in jeans and a black motorcycle club T-shirt was standing in the door of the stockroom.

"I finished shelving that new shipment," he said. He gave Joe and Frank a wary look. "There are some items we don't have out on display. I put them aside."

"Oh, thanks, Devin," Marjorie said. "That was good thinking. I'll look them over as soon as I'm done with Frank and Joe here. Devin Porter's our stock clerk," she added. "You might want to talk to him, after you finish with me."

Through the small window of the store Frank caught a glimpse of a black four-by-four as it pulled into the parking lot. Startled, he looked closer and saw three guys climbing out. A few moments later one of them opened the door. He had dark hair and he was wearing a denim jacket with cutoff sleeves and black boots. He pulled off his dark glasses and looked around.

Frank followed the direction of his gaze, just in time to see Devin give a slight nod. A moment later Devin stepped back through the door to the stock-room and closed it.

"Can I help you?" Marjorie asked.

"Naw." The guy put his sunglasses back on. As he left the store, Frank noticed a tattoo on his arm: a hawk with a machine gun in its claws.

Marjorie turned back to Joe. "As I was saying, when the factory produces more of a particular

44

model than it gets orders for, the overstock is sent over here. The customer gets a bargain, the company doesn't get stuck with a lot of unsold shoes, and everybody's happy."

Frank moved over to the window and glanced out. The black four-by-four was still there, but the guys who had been in it were nowhere in sight. Frank was positive the guy with the tattoo had given some kind of signal to Devin. Was the stock clerk in cahoots with some sort of gang?

Frank glanced over his shoulder. Marjorie was still talking to Joe. Her back was to Frank. He slipped through the door to the stockroom and paused to let his eyes get used to the darkness.

Long racks of metal shelving, loaded with boxed shoes, stretched all the way to the ceiling. The aisles between them were narrow and dark. From somewhere on the other side of the room came a few gleams of daylight and the murmur of low voices.

Frank crept closer and peered around the end of one of the racks. The sliding door to the loading dock was partly open. Devin was standing there, talking to the guy in the denim jacket.

"Look, Jerry," he said. "Why don't you come back at four, when I get off work? Not that it'll do any good. There's no way—"

"Find one," Jerry said, interrupting him. "And fast. You said you could come across with the goods, Devin. And you haven't. The boys are getting

45

impatient." He raised his voice and added, "Right, boys?"

Suddenly Frank heard a shoe scrape on the floor, right behind him. He whirled around just in time to see two guys with mean expressions come barreling through the stockroom—right toward him.

6 Joe Goes Undercover

As the two guys came for him, their fists clenched, Frank's martial-arts training took over. He put himself in a defensive stance. Then he lashed out his left foot, finding a target in his first assailant's stomach.

"Uggh!" The guy groaned and fell to his knees, clutching his stomach.

Frank got back into position, bending his knees. As soon as the second attacker came within reach, Frank grabbed the guy's outstretched arm, turned around, and threw the guy over his shoulder. The attacker went flying into a rack of shelves, then fell to the floor. Wombat sneakers came crashing down on his dazed head.

Frank was about to race from the storeroom when

something hard slammed into the back of his head. He felt himself falling, face forward. He stretched out his hands to break his fall. On the floor he turned his head. Through a haze he saw a tattooed arm help the two guys he had decked get to their feet. Three running forms darkened the open doorway. Then Frank closed his eyes, and everything around him went black.

"Hey, wake up! Come on, please. Wake up."

Frank felt himself being pulled into a sitting position. He opened his eyes and blinked. An anxious-looking face was leaning over him. After a moment Frank remembered who he was—Devin, the stock clerk at the factory outlet.

Frank reached up and carefully touched the bump on the back of his head. Whatever hit him sure had done the job.

"Can you stand up?" Devin asked nervously. "Are you okay?"

"I've been better," Frank said. "Who were those guys?"

Devin swallowed. "I tried to stop them, but they knocked me down. Listen, you won't tell anybody about this, will you? Jerry didn't mean to hurt you. He just got a little carried away. If Marjorie hears about it, I'll be fired for sure."

Instead of answering Devin's plea, Frank asked, "Who are Jerry and his friends? What did they want from you? Why did they go after me?"

Devin bit his lip nervously. "They're just some

48

guys I knew in high school. I hang out with them sometimes." He swallowed again, then cleared his throat. "They like to come on like outlaw bikers, but they're just ordinary guys. They came by to say hi and see how I was doing."

"And to jump anybody who got in their way," Frank pointed out. "That's not very friendly."

"Yeah, well . . ." Devin said, letting out a deep breath. "I guess when they saw you sneaking up on us, they freaked. Listen, you won't tell Marjorie, will you? I just got this job a couple of months ago, and I can't afford to lose it."

Frank could tell there was a lot more to the story than Devin was telling. What did Jerry mean about Devin coming across with the goods? Something crooked was going on at the store, and Devin was definitely involved. Still, there wasn't much point in getting Devin fired. He and Joe would be able to find out a lot more with Devin on the inside— especially if he owed Frank a favor.

"No, I won't say anything," Frank said finally. "But you tell your friend Jerry that he'd better watch his step. Next time I'll be ready for him."

Devin nodded glumly and started reshelving the shoes that had fallen. Frank found his way back to the showroom, where Joe and Marjorie were still in conversation.

"Hi, Frank," Joe said, looking up. "I was just asking Marjorie if she's seen any counterfeit shoes come through her store."

"I've heard it's a problem for the business as a

49

whole, sure," Marjorie replied. "But we're not really affected by it here. This is a factory outlet store. All our stock comes here directly from the Wombat warehouse. We're not like those stores that carry a dozen lines of shoes and get shipments from different places every other day."

"I see your point," Joe said. "It'd be harder to slip fakes in here than some other place."

"Right. And our inventory control system is tied directly into the Wombat Corporation computer. Every time I ring up a sale here the information is instantly transmitted to company headquarters. Any funny business would show up right away."

"What about defective shoes?" Frank asked, still feeling a little dizzy from being knocked out. He wanted to tell Joe about Devin, too, but he couldn't in front of Marjorie.

For the first time Marjorie began to look nervous. "Wombat has one of the best records for quality in the business," she said.

"You haven't seen any changes lately, though?" Joe asked.

"I can't really say anything about that," she replied. "Listen, fellows, I'd love to go on talking to you, but I've got about forty-seven different things to do."

Frank caught Joe's eye and shot a glance toward the door.

"Oh, sure, Marjorie," Joe said. "Thanks a lot for putting up with us. You've been a great help. If it's okay with you, we may come back another time with more questions, once our project gets going."

"Fine," the store manager said. "Unless I happen to be busy, I'll give you any help I can."

As soon as they were outside, Joe said, "She sure was cooperative. I doubt anything sneaky's going on here."

"Not so fast," Frank replied. "Marjorie was nice, and she seemed pretty open until we asked about defective shoes. But *something's* going on at that store, whether she knows it or not." Frank told Joe about Devin's conversation with the gang leader and the fight that followed.

Joe frowned. "I don't see how these tough guys fit into the picture."

"Me, either," Frank said. "But there's one fact I haven't mentioned yet. They were driving a black four-by-four."

Joe's frown deepened. "Eric Dresser!" he exclaimed, pounding his fist into his palm. "I *knew* he was involved in the counterfeit scheme."

"There's more than one black four-by-four in the area," Frank pointed out. "Still, Eric's job at Benlow's puts him in a key position."

Frank glanced over his shoulder. Marjorie was watching them through the window. She didn't look happy to see that they were still standing there.

"Let's talk in the van," Frank said, tossing the keys to Joe.

51

As they pulled out of the parking lot, Frank said, "The way I see it, there are two ways the crooks can get the phony Wombats into the stores. One is to pay off the stock clerk, who shelves the fakes as if they were real."

"The crooks would have to find a clerk in every store," Joe objected. "I can't believe everyone who works in sporting goods is corrupt."

"There's another possibility," Frank replied.

"Such as?"

"What if the counterfeit shoes are shipped out from the company warehouse?" Frank said. "They could be mixed in with shipments of real shoes. The stock clerks and salespeople don't even have to know that anything underhanded is going on."

"That's a possibility," Joe said. He pulled onto the expressway ramp and waited for a break in the traffic. Once they were moving again, he said, "If you're right, then the key to the operation may be the warehouse. The only way we can follow the trail of fake Wombats is to get in there."

"Exactly," Frank replied.

Joe thought for a few moments before saying, "What if one of us works undercover there, while the other one follows up on our outside leads? That way, even if our hunch isn't right, we'll still be moving on the case. The question is, can we pull it off? If the crooks are working the warehouse, won't they catch on to us?"

"That's what I've been wondering," Frank said. "Look. So far, nobody's questioned our cover story.

The crooks don't necessarily know that we're on the case. That baseball last night could have been Eric, acting on his own. As for Jerry and his gang, they may have jumped me just because I'd overheard him and Devin. That doesn't mean they're involved in the counterfeiting. Besides, they don't know we're detectives."

"Even if they do, you're the only one they really saw," Joe added. "So it looks as if I'm the one who should work undercover, just in case."

Once they got home, Frank put in a call to Karla Newhouse. When she was on the line, he told her his idea and asked her if she could get Joe a job at the warehouse.

"I don't know if I can do that," Karla replied in an unhappy voice. "The people over in personnel don't like it when someone tries to pull strings. And I'm pretty new here, you know. I have to be careful not to step on people's toes."

Patiently Frank said, "I can understand that. But I'd appreciate it if you could try. Joe and I are doing an investigation that may affect the whole future of the company. Getting Joe into the warehouse is important to our investigation."

After a short silence Newhouse said, "I'll see what I can do and get back to you." She hung up before Frank could say goodbye.

An hour later the phone rang. Joe picked it up.

"Welcome to Wombat," Karla said. "Report to the warehouse foreman, Lincoln Metairie, at eight tomorrow morning. I told him you're part of a new trainee program for high school students. This had better be worthwhile," she added. "I had to call in a few favors to swing it."

"Thanks," Joe said. "We'll keep you posted."

He hung up and turned to Frank. "I got the job," he reported. "I start tomorrow. How should we spend my last free night before I join the working world?"

"We could buy a pizza and rent a movie," Frank suggested.

"You're on," Joe said, reaching for his jacket.

The next morning Frank drove Joe to Holman Heights to his new job. The Wombat warehouse was in the same industrial park as the factory outlet. Frank stopped a block from the plant entrance.

"It's better if nobody sees us together," he said. "Why don't you meet me here at noon? We can grab some lunch and catch up on what's happening."

"Sure thing," Joe replied. "See you then."

Joe hiked across a crowded parking lot toward the factory. It was a modern two-story building with a big electric sign on the roof that read WOMBAT—Shoe of Champions. The warehouse, which was attached to one side of the factory, looked at least as big as a football field.

Joe found the employees' entrance at five minutes

54

to eight. He climbed a narrow flight of metal stairs and went inside. A uniformed security guard was sitting on a high stool next to the time clock. He took Joe's name, checked it against a list on his clipboard, and directed him to the foreman's office.

Two men were standing just inside the glass-walled office. One of them, a hefty, broad-shouldered man in his early forties, looked up when Joe walked in.

"Mr. Metairie?" Joe asked.

"That's me," the man said. "You must be the kid I got the call about. You're going to be working here a couple of weeks, right?"

"Yes, sir. My name's Joe Hardy."

"Okay. And don't 'sir' me, Joe. It makes me nervous. Have you ever worked with computers or driven a forklift?"

"I'm no expert, but I've done both," Joe said.

The foreman looked at him skeptically for a moment, then nodded. "Okay, we'll see. This is Ray Beane, our dispatcher. He'll show you around and get you started."

Ray was a wiry-looking man in his early thirties with a bushy blond mustache. As he led Joe out of the office, he stopped to pick up a diagram.

"This is a map of the warehouse," he explained, handing it to Joe. "Don't lose it. You're going to need it."

Within two minutes Joe understood what Ray had

meant. The warehouse was a maze of eight-foot-wide aisles, each of them lined with stacks of big cartons that stretched high over his head.

"Two things happen here," Ray explained as they turned into still another aisle. "We take in shoes from the factory next door, and we send out shoes to distributors and stores. Linc said you should work with me on fulfillment."

"What's that?" Joe asked.

"Taking care of orders," Ray replied. "The way it works, we get a printout of an order and check it against the computer to find out if we have it in stock and where it is. Then we go out and get the items and package them for shipment. Those cartons hold two dozen pairs each, so they're pretty heavy. Don't try to lift them by yourself. That's what we've got forklifts for. I'll—"

He broke off as the beeper on his belt sounded.

"I'll be back in a minute," he told Joe. "You take a look around and get used to the place."

Alone, Joe read the numbers painted on the shelf nearest him, then checked his diagram of the warehouse. If he understood the system—and he wasn't at all sure that he did—he was three aisles away from the north end of the warehouse. And the office and entrance were somewhere behind him and to the left.

He was headed for the nearest intersection when a slight noise caught his ear. It had come from the other side of the wall of cartons on his right. He

56

glanced up and let out a gasp. One column of the heavy cartons was no longer upright. It was leaning over, farther and farther, and the cartons at the top were starting to slide off the stack. In another instant they would topple over and crush Joe under their weight!

7 Dirty Tricks

As the heavy cartons of shoes started to fall, Joe took a quick step backward, then another. But his heel caught on a crooked floorboard, and he felt himself falling. On instinct, Joe tucked his chin against his chest and rolled to one side, then wrapped his arms around his head.

The cartons bounced off the opposite rack of shelving and smashed to the floor—well away from where Joe was crouched. The loud crash echoed throughout the warehouse.

Joe got to his feet. He looked up at the high shelves. The cartons hadn't toppled on their own. Somebody must have pushed them, from the next aisle.

From nearby came the sound of footsteps running

toward him. Ray Beane, white-faced, appeared at the end of the aisle. "What happened?" he demanded. "Are you all right?"

Joe took a deep breath. "I'm okay," he said. "I don't know what happened. Those cartons just fell over."

Ray looked at the cartons in the aisle, then turned back to Joe, a doubting expression on his face. "Did you try to move one of them?" he asked.

"No, I didn't," Joe insisted. "I didn't even touch them."

"What's all this?" a new voice demanded. It was Lincoln Metairie, the warehouse foreman. "What on earth happened here?"

"The cartons must have been stacked badly," Ray answered. "They fell over and almost landed on Joe."

The foreman frowned. "Hmmph," he grunted. "I told the main office they were making a mistake, sending an inexperienced kid in here. A warehouse can be a dangerous place if you don't know what you're doing. People get hurt all the time."

As he said this, he gave Joe a narrow-eyed look. Were his words just a warning? Joe wondered. Or were they meant as a threat?

"Okay, enough gab," Lincoln continued, turning to Ray. "Clear up this mess, then you and Joe can start assembling this morning's orders."

As the foreman walked away, Joe studied him. *Someone* had pushed those cartons over, Joe was sure of that. As far as Joe knew, the only people who knew that he was in the warehouse were Lincoln and Ray.

"Okay, Joe, you heard the man," Ray said. "I'll get a forklift and we'll put these boxes back where they belong. Maybe this time they'll stay where they're put."

As Joe helped Ray stack up the cartons, he said, "I still don't understand why they fell like that." He put both hands on the sides of one of the cartons and shoved at it.

"Hey, what are you doing?" Ray demanded in alarm. "You want to upset the whole stack again?"

"No, look," Joe replied. "I can't even budge it. And I'm no weakling, either. Listen, Ray. I've heard that in some places the guys like to play tricks on newcomers. Do you think somebody might have pushed over these cartons on purpose, to give me a scare?"

Ray frowned. "I never thought of that," he said. "It could be, I guess." He paused, then nodded his head. "Sure, that must be it. The whole thing was some stupid practical joke. Let's just hope it doesn't go any further. Now come on. We've got a lot of work to do before lunch."

When Frank got to the Wombat Corporation headquarters, the same receptionist from the day before was on duty. He looked at Frank without any sign of recognition and said, "Can I help you?"

"Mr. Brinkstead, please," Frank replied. "My name's Frank Hardy."

The receptionist looked doubtfully at Frank's polo shirt, jeans, and running shoes, then said, "His line is busy. Is he expecting you?"

"No, but he'll want to see me."

With a sniff the receptionist said, "Have a seat. I'll tell Mr. Brinkstead's secretary you're here."

The receptionist took his time letting Brinkstead know Frank was waiting. Within a few minutes Winston Brinkstead appeared in the doorway. The heavyset man looked as if he had been having a bad morning. "Come on in, Frank," he said. He led the way to his office and carefully closed the door, then added, "How is the investigation going? Are you and your brother making any progress?"

"Definitely," Frank replied. "But I need to check out some of our ideas. I'd like to spend some time going over your sales records for the last few weeks."

Brinkstead's manner cooled. "You have to realize that is highly sensitive information," he said.

"I know," Frank said. "But this is a very sensitive problem we're working on. You're already trusting us to work on it. So you might as well trust us all the way."

The Wombat vice president chewed on his lower lip for a moment, then said, "You're right. I'll have my secretary find you a free terminal and show you the ropes."

Frank spent the rest of the morning sitting at a computer terminal, scanning columns of numbers and copying some of them into his notebook. The company kept very thorough records, not just of the orders that each store placed, but of returns and reported sales as well.

When he came to the file on Benlow's, Frank studied it very carefully. After twenty minutes he did some calculations on the numbers he had copied down. He looked at the result, sat back, and let out a low whistle.

He glanced at his watch. It was almost time to pick up Joe for lunch. Frank was going to have some amazing news for him.

"You fellows ready to order?" the waitress asked.

Frank glanced at the menu and said, "I'll have a BLT, fries, and a large soda."

Joe said, "Make mine a cheeseburger deluxe and a glass of milk."

The waitress took their menus and went to turn in the order. Joe glanced around. The old-fashioned diner had a long row of booths covered in blue plastic next to the front windows. The stools at the counter were in matching blue plastic. This was the only restaurant close to the industrial park. It was barely noon, but almost every booth and stool was already taken.

"I'll be right back," Joe told Frank. "I'm going to wash up. I feel pretty grimy after this morning's work."

"Don't be long," Frank replied. "I've found a few things out this morning that I want to tell you about."

"So have I."

The door to the men's room was near the entrance to the kitchen, behind a pillar covered with plastic ivy. Joe washed his hands, dried them under the hot-air blower, and pulled the door open. As he did, he heard a sudden clatter of dishes. A woman's voice said, "Oh, sorry. I didn't see you there."

For a moment Joe thought she was talking to him. Then a gruff man's voice said, "My fault. I wasn't watching where I was going."

Joe looked over. The waitress was standing a few feet away, in the doorway to the kitchen. She had a tray of orders balanced on her left arm. With her right hand, she was rearranging the dishes on the tray.

She turned her head to say something to the cook. As she did, a hand snaked out from behind the ivy-covered pillar and quickly poured something into the dark liquid in one of the glasses on the tray.

For a moment Joe was too astonished to move. Someone had just doped one of the drinks! But who did it, and who was it meant for? He had to find out. He darted forward. But at that same moment the waitress turned and started toward the dining room. Joe had to stop short to keep from bumping into her and knocking over her tray. By the time the way was clear, the guy on the other side of the pillar had gotten away. Joe saw him dart out the door. He wanted to follow him but knew he had to find out who the drink was going to.

63

Joe followed the waitress. She weaved through the tables to the booth where Frank was waiting. She set down a burger platter, a sandwich, and a plate of fries. Then she added two glasses, one of milk and one of cola. Frank smiled at her and reached for the cola.

To his horror, Joe realized it was the same glass that he'd just seen someone dose!

8 Sneaky Business

"Frank!" Joe shouted. He dashed toward the booth, at a speed just short of a run. "Frank, wait!"

Frank looked up and paused, with the glass still in his hand. The waitress turned around with a puzzled expression. People at the other tables looked up, startled by Joe's cry.

Joe reached the booth and leaned over to take the glass from Frank's hand. "Order another soda," he said quietly. "I'd like to take this one home."

Frank gave him a curious look. Then his eyes widened. Turning to the waitress, he said, "Another cola, please. And could we also have an empty cup and a lid?"

"Sure," the waitress said with a shrug.

When she left, Joe quickly went to the window to see if he could find the man who ran away. He saw no trace of him or a car leaving. With an exasperated sigh he went back to his brother and explained what had happened. Frank took the glass from Joe and sniffed it, then set it down carefully on the table. "Did you get a good look at the person who did it?" he asked.

Joe made a face. "Just his hand and part of his arm. Fairly large, fairly tanned, with fairly dark hair. I do know he's probably a leftie. At least, he poured with his left hand, and he wasn't wearing a watch on that wrist."

"Hmmm," Frank said. The waitress came by with an empty paper cup with a plastic lid and a fresh soda. After she left, Frank said, "I get the feeling that our cover is blown."

Joe paused with his burger in his hand. "I've had that feeling all morning," he said. He told Frank about the falling cartons. "Anybody in the warehouse could have pushed them over, but the obvious suspects are Linc, the foreman, and Ray, the dispatcher. So far they're the only two people who know I'm working in the warehouse."

"If either of them is involved in the phony Wombat racket, he'd have a good reason for trying to scare you off . . . or worse," Frank said.

Joe nodded thoughtfully. "Either one of them is in a good spot to be part of the gang," he said. "Linc is in charge of the whole warehousing operation, and Ray is the one who actually ships shoes to the stores. What I don't understand is how they caught on to me so fast."

"Maybe they didn't," Frank suggested.

"Those cartons didn't fall over on their own," Joe retorted.

"No, what I mean is, maybe the one who's mixed up in the racket is simply nervous and suspicious," Frank said. "This morning you show up as part of a trainee program that no one's ever heard of before. He may not know you're a detective, but why take a chance? He decided to get you out of the picture, one way or another."

Joe raised his eyebrows. "Even to the point of trying to poison me or the guy I'm having lunch with? That's pretty drastic."

"I know," Frank said. "But we're dealing with an important operation here. I spent the morning going over the records of sales and returns. I found out that until a couple of months ago, there were hardly any returns of defective shoes. Since then the number has been climbing steeply every week. By last week it was up to over three hundred pairs, almost all of them from stores in this area. At fifty bucks a pair, wholesale, that's fifteen thousand dollars in one week."

"Were all of them counterfeit?" Joe asked.

"The records don't say," Frank replied. "That's one of the things we have to check out. But there's something else to keep in mind, too. The only counterfeits that we know about are the ones that came back because they were defective. What

67

about the ones that aren't? For every phony Wombat we know about, there could be ten others out there on people's feet. We could be talking about millions of dollars in illegal profits."

"A crook would do a lot to protect that kind of money," Joe said. "We'd better watch our step."

Frank checked his watch. "When do you have to be back at work? One? Let's finish eating and run over to Wombat headquarters. We should have just enough time to catch Karla Newhouse and ask her a couple of questions."

The Hardys quickly finished their lunch and paid the check. They left the restaurant with the dosed soda in a take-out paper cup and headed for the Wombat headquarters. When they entered the office building, Frank saw with relief that the receptionist was not at his desk. "Come on," he told Joe, heading for the inner door.

Once inside, they paused and tried to remember the way to Karla Newhouse's office. At that moment a young guy pushing a mail cart came along and directed them to the right.

There was no one at the secretary's desk outside Karla's office. The door to the inner office was ajar. Frank tapped lightly on the door and looked inside.

The Wombat vice president was standing next to the desk with her back to the door. She had the telephone in her hand. She glanced around and saw Frank. A look of alarm flashed across her face. She said something quickly into the telephone and hung up. Then she turned to face Frank and Joe.

"Sorry to bother you again," Frank said. "The investigation is going well, but we'd like more information."

"Oh?" she said. "What sort of information?"

"Does your office keep a file of complaint letters from customers?"

Karla paused, weighing her response. "Yes, of course," she finally said. "Why?"

"Would you mind giving us copies of the letters for the last six weeks or so?" Frank continued. "We're hoping to spot a pattern in the complaints that will help us pinpoint the source of the counter-feit shoes."

The Wombat official hesitated again. "Those letters are confidential material," she said. "If one of our competitors got hold of them . . ." The idea made her shudder.

"We'll guard them carefully," Joe promised. "Besides, they can't be any more confidential than the information we already have."

"That's a point," Karla conceded. "Well, how soon do you need them?"

"Right away, if possible," Frank replied.

"Hmmm . . . my secretary has the afternoon off, and I wouldn't want to trust this material to the people in the photocopy room."

She glanced at her watch. "I'll tell you what. If you have a few minutes, I'll take the file down the hall and copy it myself."

"Thanks a lot," Frank said.

She unlocked a file cabinet in the outer office and

pulled out a thick folder. "I won't be long," she said. "Make yourselves comfortable."

Once she was out of sight, Joe said, "She seems awfully nervous. Do you think she could have anything to do with the counterfeiting scheme?"

Frank frowned. "It's possible," he said. "That would certainly explain how the gang has been able to keep track of our moves so well. But then, why would she agree to let us see those letters?"

"Maybe she knows they won't help us," Joe suggested.

Frank went over to Karla's desk and began scanning the papers on it. "Well, well, well," he said. "Check it out. Here's a memo about the counterfeiting," he reported. He gave a low whistle. "She claims the phony Wombats cost the company over fifty thousand dollars last month, just in returns."

"Does she offer any ideas for what to do about it?" Joe asked.

Frank read on. "She thinks the company ought to go public with the problem. She says the new management team has to mount a major campaign —check all the shoes that are already in stores, confiscate the counterfeits, and add features to the shoes that will be harder to fake."

Joe, in turn, whistled. "That'd cost a fortune!" he exclaimed. "Still, I guess it's better than letting the company go down the tubes."

"She says the same thing, but in classier language," Frank said with a grin. "It's interesting, though—the memo doesn't say a word about a campaign to find out who's behind the counterfeiting."

"That's strange," Joe remarked. "Unless the gang is unmasked, what's to keep them from making more phony Wombats? They obviously have good sources of inside information. How long would it take them to copy whatever new features the company comes up with?"

"It does seem like a pretty obvious point for a top executive like Karla Newhouse to overlook," Frank said. "Unless she had some reason to play it down. Remember, she wasn't so hot to have us investigate. Maybe she has something to hide."

"I'd sure like to know who she was talking to on the phone when we came in," Joe said. "She hung up pretty fast."

Frank was still looking over the papers on top of the desk. He glanced over at the telephone and said, "Hey, wait, maybe we can find out. Her phone has a redial feature. As long as she was the one to make the call—"

Frank picked up the receiver and pressed the redial button. He heard a sequence of tones, a brief ring, and then a male voice said, "Did you get rid of them?"

Frank was sure that he had heard that voice before, but where?

"Good afternoon, sir," he said smoothly. "This is telephone repair. We've been doing maintenance

71

on this line, and we want to make sure that everything has been reconnected properly. Can you confirm your telephone number for us?"

"Huh? Oh, sure," the man said and told Frank the number.

Frank scribbled the number on a scrap of paper, then continued. "And how is that listed? What is the name of the subscriber?"

"This is the Wombat Factory Outlet Store," the man said. "Is that what you mean?"

"Yes, thank you," Frank said. "Yes, that's just what our records show. Have you experienced any problems with your line in the last half hour or so, while we were working on it? Any static or interference with calls?"

"No, nothing like that. It worked just fine."

"You did use it, though?" Frank pursued. "And you didn't have any problems? Good. Is there anyone else at this number who might have had difficulties?"

"No, I'm here alone," the man said. "Everyone else is out to lunch." A note of suspicion crept into his voice. "Say, do you really need to ask all these questions?"

"Yes, sir, and we appreciate your taking the time to answer them," Frank said quickly. "You can understand that we want to avoid inconveniencing our customers. Your cooperation will help us in that effort. May I ask your name for my report?"

"My name? I'm Devin Porter. But listen, I just work here, I don't want—"

72

"Well, thanks for your help, Mr. Porter," Frank said, interrupting him.

Suddenly Joe tapped Frank's arm and pointed urgently toward the office door. Frank looked over and saw that it was open a crack. "Sorry to bother you, sir," he said quickly, and hung up.

The door swung open. Karla Newhouse came in with a stack of photocopies in her hand and a look of deep suspicion on her face.

"What are you doing with my telephone?" she demanded. "Who were you talking to? Answer me, at once!"

9 A Clever Operation

Karla glared at Frank and repeated, "Answer me. Why were you using my telephone and who were you talking to?"

"Just a guy who's fixing my camera," Frank said, thinking on his feet. He stepped away from behind her desk. "I'm sorry. While you were gone, I remembered that I'd promised to call him today. I didn't think you'd mind."

"Well, I do mind," Karla replied. "I could have sensitive documents on my desk. What if you and your brother were actually spies for another company, or for someone who's out to get me?"

"We're not," Joe insisted. "You have to believe we're trying to help you."

The Wombat vice president bit her lower lip as

she looked from Joe to Frank. "I didn't mean to accuse you," she finally said in a calmer voice, "but I'm sure you can see why I was upset. Here," she added, handing Frank the copies of customer complaints that had been sent to Wombat. "You'll be careful with these, won't you? In the wrong hands, this stuff would be dynamite."

"We'll take good care of it," Frank promised.

Joe glanced at his watch. "Uh-oh, we'd better go," he said. "I'm going to be late getting back to work. And it's my first day on the job, too!"

As they hurried across the parking lot toward the van, Frank filled Joe in on the phone call. He started up the van and added, "Devin must have thought I was Karla calling him back. The first words he said when he picked up the phone were, 'Did you get rid of them?' Three guesses who he was talking about."

Joe nodded. "So Devin Porter and Karla Newhouse know each other. Wombat's vice president for customer relations and the new stock clerk at the company's factory outlet—whatever the connection is, I'm willing to bet that it isn't on the up-and-up."

"Don't forget about Devin's so-called friends who tried to jump me yesterday," Frank pointed out. "It appears Devin deserves a closer look."

"Why don't you go by there after you drop me off?" Joe suggested. "You can say you have a few more questions for our class project."

Frank made a right turn at the industrial park and

followed the signs to the Wombat factory. In the big field next to the plant a bunch of guys had just finished a game of baseball. Some of them were already walking back to the plant, carrying bats and mitts.

"The place seems pretty loose about lunch hours," Frank remarked, after a glance at his watch. "I'll drop you off here so no one makes the connection between us. We may still have a little cover left," he joked.

Frank pulled over. Joe climbed out and shut the door, then put his head in the window to say, "I'll wait for you here, at around five."

Joe watched Frank drive off and then glanced around. The guys who had been playing baseball in the field were all inside now. Joe walked quickly across the lot to the warehouse entrance. The guard on duty was different from the one that morning. He gave Joe a friendly nod and went back to looking at his magazine.

Joe found his time card and put it in the slot of the clock at 1:07. As it clicked, a hand fell on his shoulder.

"I hope you had a nice, leisurely lunch, Hardy," Lincoln Metairie said. "I'm sorry you had to cut it short for something so dumb as a job."

"I'm sorry I'm late—" Joe began.

The foreman interrupted him. "Never mind that. Go over and give Ray a hand. We had a bunch of orders come in at noon."

For the next two hours Joe was too busy working

76

to give a thought to the investigation. He raced up and down the aisles of the warehouse on his forklift, gathering cartons Ray told him to find. Then he took them back to the dispatcher's station. There, the shipping labels were put on and the cartons were stacked in one of the big trailers waiting at the loading dock.

"I can't believe some of these orders," Joe said to Ray at one point. "I mean, a whole carton of black referee shoes in size eight? How long does it take a store to sell that many?"

"These orders aren't going to stores," Ray explained. "They're being shipped to distributors in different parts of the country. They're the ones who fill individual orders. We'd go crazy trying to put together separate orders from all the thousands of stores that carry Wombats."

Joe glanced down at the bill of lading. It was addressed to Abaco Distrib., Inc., in Missouri City, Texas. Joe frowned. If it was the distributors who supplied the stores, then they would have to be in on the counterfeiting scheme, too. Otherwise, how could the crooks be sure which stores were getting the counterfeits? And how would they collect the money for them? It would be a complicated scheme to run all the fake shoes out of one warehouse.

Ray rubbed his chin and added, "We used to do all the distribution ourselves, when the company was smaller. Let me tell you, it was a nightmare. It's bad enough that we still do it for the stores in this sales area. You'll see what I mean tomorrow when we have to fill an order from Sportshoes Limited. One pair of this, two pairs of that—it drives you nuts."

The dispatcher turned back to his computer screen and pressed a few keys. "Wouldn't you know it," he muttered. "We're missing a couple of cartons of Helio-Springs for an order from St. Louis. I'll bet they've got them sitting over in the factory and just haven't gotten around to letting us know."

Ray grabbed a pad and scribbled a note, then tore it out and handed it to Joe. "Here," he said, "take this over to Norm Weiss, in production. Tell him I need quick action on it."

"How do I find him?" Joe asked.

"He's usually at the far end of the line, near the quality control station. Ask anybody."

All day Joe had been hoping for an excuse to look around the factory. Now that Ray had given him one, he took full advantage of it. He wandered around the big, noisy space, trying to figure out how the shoes were made.

At one end workers were taking brightly colored leather hides, stamping patterns on them, and cutting them out with electric knives. The pieces of leather were then sorted into trays and carried along to stitching machines. Before Joe's eyes, the different bits of leather took on the shape of the upper part of an athletic shoe. This is all pretty amazing, Joe thought.

"Hey, kid, are you looking for somebody?" a burly man in a hard hat demanded.

78

"Um, yes I am. Norm Weiss," Joe replied. "I've got a message for him from Ray Beane."

"You're in the wrong place, kid," the man said gruffly. He pointed to the far side of the factory floor. "Try over near quality control. They'll know where he is."

"Thanks," Joe said, walking in the direction the guy had pointed. Over his shoulder he saw the man in the hard hat was still standing in the same place, watching him. Joe gave him a halfhearted smile and continued toward quality control.

When he got to the other side of the factory, Joe found half a dozen workers in white overalls, sitting at workbenches. Next to each was a wheeled rack full of small plastic bins. Each bin contained a newly made pair of Wombat athletic shoes.

Joe stopped by the nearest workbench to watch. The inspector grabbed a bin, pulled out one of the two shoes in it, and looked at it through a magnifying lens clipped to his glasses. He tugged at the shoe's upper and each of the seams, then studied the inside under a bright lamp. After doing the same with the other of the pair, he picked up a gadget that looked like a big pair of pliers, fitted the edge of one of the shoes between the jaws, and squeezed. A moment later the shoes disappeared down a conveyor belt. The inspector was already examining another pair of shoes.

"Are you the kid who's looking for me?" a voice said near Joe's ear.

Joe jumped and looked around. The man stand-

79

ing next to him had bushy gray eyebrows and little tufts of graying hair sticking out over his ears.

"Norm Weiss?" Joe asked. The man nodded. "Ray Beane sent me over with this note," Joe continued. "Something about finding some cartons of Helio-Springs for St. Louis."

Weiss looked at the note, wiggled his eyebrows, and said, "Tell him I'll do what I can."

He noticed Joe glancing back at the inspector's workbench and added, "First time you've seen all this?"

"Yes, it is," Joe admitted.

"What you see here is the next to last step," Weiss explained. "Most factories just check out a few of their shoes, picked off the assembly line. Not here. Our inspectors look over every single shoe we make. They don't put their stamp on it unless they're sure it's okay. Any inspector who lets more than a very few defective shoes get by him doesn't keep his job very long."

"That gizmo that looks like pliers must be the stamp, right?" Joe said.

"Right. Each inspector has his own, and you can bet that he doesn't go lending it out to his friends. Every time he passes a shoe, he's putting his career on the line."

"It's a pretty thorough system," Joe said.

"The best in the business," Weiss replied. "It has to be. One of the biggest reasons that Wombat got to be a top brand is that our customers know we make all our own shoes, right here, and inspect every one of them. They know they won't get stuck with an inferior or defective product."

Joe wondered if Weiss knew about all the defective shoes on the market under the Wombat name. Probably not, since he was bragging about how good the quality control was.

Weiss waved his hand at the factory floor. "We've got one of the most advanced automated production lines in the business," he added. "In a pinch a half dozen people could probably run it. But we believe in giving every pair of Wombats individual attention, all the same."

It occurred to Joe that the Wombat Corporation ought to make some commercials starring Norm Weiss. He obviously believed every word he was saying.

"I'd better get back," Joe said. "Ray must be wondering what happened to me."

Weiss laughed. "Just tell him I wouldn't stop bending your ear," he said. "He knows me well enough to know that it's the truth!"

Frank finished reading another of the complaint letters that Karla had copied for him. He shifted it from the top to the bottom of the stack. It was just as he had thought when he studied the computerized sales records. Practically all of the serious complaints were from towns in the Bayport area. There were a few letters from other parts of the country, but they were about shoes that didn't perform as well as expected, not about shoes that fell apart.

81

Frank had parked the van in the lot of a pottery discount store, just across the road from the Wombat Factory Outlet. Frank looked up at the storefront, then checked his watch. Five minutes to four. If he remembered right, Devin got off work at four. Ten more minutes.

Frank looked down at the next letter and chuckled. A kid in Nebraska had a complaint. Right after he bought a pair of Wombat Champions, his basketball team lost the all-county championship. He wanted to know how the company had the nerve to call their basketball shoes Champions.

When Frank glanced up again, a kid with black hair, jeans, and a motorcycle jacket was coming out the door of the outlet store. Frank recognized Devin at once. The young stock clerk walked over to a battered old sedan and climbed in. Frank turned his ignition key and started the van's engine. He let Devin get a half-block lead, then pulled out after him.

Devin led Frank across the railroad tracks to a section of Holman Heights called the Valley. He turned onto a street lined with old three-story apartment houses. The buildings had outside staircases and open porches at each floor. A few of them were freshly painted, but the rest were run-down.

Halfway down the block Devin pulled up to the curb and got out. He walked across to one of the houses and mounted the stairs to the third floor. Frank waited a few minutes to give him time to go

82

inside. Then he got out of the van, went over to the house, and read the names on the mailboxes.

The third-floor apartment was occupied by Ms. Donna Newhouse-Porter.

Frank stared at the name. Newhouse-Porter? He had been wondering why Karla Newhouse had been telephoning Devin Porter. Now he knew. Unless this was a bizarre coincidence, which he didn't believe for a moment, they were related!

The question was: Were they only relatives, or were they also partners in crime?

10 Stalking a Suspect

Frank glanced up the outside stairway. Should he confront Devin? He didn't have any proof that Devin was involved in distributing fake Wombats, or that Karla was helping him.

While Frank was trying to decide what to do, he caught a glimpse of a familiar-looking black four-by-four going past. That made up his mind for him. He dashed back to the van and followed.

The four-by-four led him through the residential neighborhood. Soon, though, Frank was following the driver into Holman Heights's business district. The four-by-four turned right at a busy intersection and parked in front of a block of stores. Frank moved forward, almost to the crosswalk, and stopped with all but the front of the van hidden by the building on the corner. He could see a candy store, a dry cleaner, a small grocery, a videotape rental, and a pizza place. He reached into the glove compartment and pulled out a pair of small but powerful binoculars.

Three guys climbed out of the four-by-four. They stood talking on the sidewalk for a moment, then went into the pizza place, which was called Angelo's. Frank had time to get a good look at them through the binoculars. Not that he needed it. He had recognized them even before they got out of the auto. They were Jerry and his two buddies—the same guys who had tried to jump him at the outlet the day before.

Frank slumped down in his seat and watched the door of the pizzeria. For fifteen minutes or so nothing at all happened. Finally the door to the pizzeria opened. Jerry and his friends came out, climbed into the four-by-four, and started down the street in a squeal of tires. Frank reached for the ignition key, then took his hand away and sat back. He waited a few minutes, then got out of the van and walked around the corner to the pizzeria. Frank pulled open the door and went inside.

The place was empty, except for a man with a gray mustache and sagging cheeks who stood behind the counter. He was stretching out a ball of pizza dough. The man looked around and nodded to Frank. "Can I help you?"

"A slice with mushrooms and a cola, please,"

Frank said. He pulled out a stool and sat down at the counter.

"Coming right up." The man took a slice of pizza from the pan on the counter, sprinkled a handful of mushrooms over it, and slid it into the oven. Then he filled a glass with ice and soda and put it on the counter in front of Frank.

"Are you Angelo?" Frank asked.

"That's right," the man said.

"I thought so. A guy I know said you make the best pizza around here."

"That's nice to hear," the man said, dusting his hands off on his apron. "Who said so?"

"Devin's his name," Frank replied casually. "He lives around here, I think."

"Devin Porter? Skinny kid with black hair? Sure, he's been coming in here since he was too little to reach the counter. He lives over on Buford Street. You a friend of his?"

"We just met recently," Frank said carefully. "I don't know him well."

"He's a good kid," Angelo said. "But then he got in with a bad crowd. That Jerry Dresser and his hoodlum friends. They're the ones to blame for Devin's trouble with the cops last year."

"Trouble?" Frank asked, all ears.

A look of concern crossed Angelo's face. Then he said, "Hey, it's no secret, and anyway, it's over and done with. Devin borrowed a car from a neighbor and forgot to ask first, that's all. It was just bad luck that he got pulled over."

86

"What happened then?" Frank asked.

Angelo shrugged. "It all worked out. The guy who owned the car wouldn't file charges. Gave Devin a real scare, though. His poor mother about had a heart attack, her only kid being called a thief. Since then he's got a job and started hanging out with a better crowd. I hope it lasts."

Angelo took a long-handled wooden paddle and slid Frank's slice of pizza out of the oven onto a plate. "Here you go," he said. "Enjoy."

"Thanks." Something Angelo had said was bothering Frank. He took a couple of bites of the pizza and a sip of soda, then said, "Did you say the leader of the crowd Devin hooked up with is named Dresser? I know someone by that name who's from around here, but it can't be the same guy. The guy I know is in high school, and he's a track star."

Angelo took a cloth and wiped the counter. "That's Eric you're thinking of," he said. "Jerry's kid brother. He's won medals and all. If he keeps it up, he's got a good shot at winning a scholarship to go to college. Unless he hangs around that no-good brother of his too much and blows it."

A bunch of junior high school kids came in and slid two tables together to make enough room for all of them. Angelo went over to take their orders. Frank finished his slice of pizza and put his money on the counter.

"See you," Frank called to Angelo as he headed for the door. The pizzeria owner gave him a wave.

The Wombat factory and warehouse was just a

87

ten-minute drive away. Joe was already waiting outside the gate when Frank pulled up. As soon as Joe climbed in the van, Frank started telling him about the link between Karla Newhouse and Devin Porter.

"So Karla might be the boss of this racket, and Devin is her guy on the spot," Joe suggested.

"Maybe," Frank replied. "But wait—there's more. That guy who jumped me yesterday turns out to be Eric Dresser's older brother."

After mulling over this news for a few moments, Joe said, "All right! This whole thing is starting to come together. Karla is an important executive at Wombat, but she's part of this new management team. Maybe her job isn't that safe. So she invents this scheme to make herself a lot of money on the side—just in case she's fired. She brings in Devin and Eric. They're both stock clerks for Wombat dealers. They're in a perfect position to get the fake shoes into circulation. Eric's brother and his friends supply the muscle for the operation. Is that what you were thinking?"

"Pretty much so," Frank said. "But we've still got a bunch of loose ends to tie up. For instance, you said Karla is making herself a nest egg. How, exactly?"

"By selling the counterfeit shoes, of course," Joe answered.

"Okay. Explain how the money gets to her. She's not peddling them herself. Somewhere along the line, somebody has to pass money to her or her gang. Who? How?"

"I get your point," Joe said with a frown. "She can't exactly send out invoices, either."

"Nope," Frank said. "Also—explain who dosed my drink at lunch. You're sure it was a man's arm?"

"Well . . . call it ninety-nine percent sure," Joe replied. "So it wasn't Karla. It could have been some man who's working with her. Like Devin, or Eric, or some guy in Eric's brother's gang."

"True," Frank said. He turned into the driveway of their house and parked.

"Another thing—those cartons that nearly fell on you this morning," Frank continued. "There's no reason to think that any of those people—Devin, Karla, Eric, or Eric's brother—were at the warehouse this morning."

Joe shrugged. "Obviously somebody at the warehouse is part of the racket. Linc Metairie or Ray Beane, for instance. They both knew where I was. Maybe when Karla called to set up my job, she told them to try to scare me off."

The paper cup of dosed cola was still sitting in the drink holder of the van's console. Frank picked it up and said, "Let's run some tests on this after dinner. I'd like to know exactly what somebody was planning for me to drink with my lunch."

Mr. and Mrs. Hardy, along with Aunt Gertrude, were attending a fund-raiser that evening, so Joe and Frank had the house to themselves. They drew

89

straws to see who would cook, and Joe lost. He made a quick dinner of spaghetti and bottled sauce, and the two brothers ate quickly.

After washing up, they went downstairs to their crime lab. Joe used an eyedropper to place tiny quantities of the cola in each of a rack of test tubes. Then he poured what was left into a sterile beaker, sealed it, and labeled it. Meanwhile, Frank took down their kit of chemicals. With these they would be able to detect the presence of any of the fifty most common poisons and hazardous substances.

They hadn't used the poisons kit in a while. Joe read from the manual while Frank carried out each of the steps and took notes on what happened. After an hour and a half of work they studied the results.

"Aside from caffeine, which must have been from the cola itself," Joe announced, "the closest match is some form of aniline dye. It's listed as being hazardous but not fatal in small quantities."

"In other words," Frank said, "if I had drunk it, I might have turned purple but I wouldn't have died. I can't tell you how much better I feel to hear that."

Frank went over to the bookcase and pulled down a chemical reference dictionary. "Aniline dyes," he read. "A bunch of formulas . . . developed in nineteenth century, blah blah . . . used principally in dying fabrics and leather."

"*Leather?*" Joe repeated, shooting Frank a glance. "As in brightly colored athletic shoes, for example?"

"Could be," Frank said. "Which means your

buddies at the Wombat factory are still very much in the running."

Frank suddenly heard a noise. "Did you just hear something outside?" he demanded after a moment.

Joe was still for a second, then shook his head. "I don't think so," he said. "What kind of noise?"

At that instant something rattled against one of the windows on the ground floor, as if someone had tossed a handful of gravel. Joe met Frank's eyes.

"We'd better go look," he said.

At the top of the cellar stairs Frank said in a low voice, "Let's sneak out the back door and come at them from both directions."

"Okay," Joe replied. At the kitchen door he tapped Frank's shoulder, then pointed to the left. Frank gave an abrupt nod and ran quietly in the direction of the rosebushes. Joe watched for a moment, then turned and crept toward the driveway.

The street lamps were on, but the nearest one was on the other side of the oak tree in front of the house next door. A light breeze swayed the branches, casting weird shadows on the driveway. But some of the dark forms stayed the same—the azalea bush on one side of the drive, the small spruce on the other—and the four-by-four that was parked, facing out, in the driveway.

His senses sharpened, Joe took a step forward, looking in every direction for the intruders he knew must be nearby. Nothing seemed to move. He took another step forward.

91

A tiny spark of light from the driver's side of the four-by-four was followed by the sound of the starter cranking. The engine caught and the car started to move. Joe began to run toward it. Suddenly a shape loomed up in front of him. He dodged to the left, but a loop of rope tightened around his chest and arms, right at the elbow.

"I got one of them!" a voice shouted. "Here I come—move out!"

The engine roared. Before he could do anything to save himself, Joe was jerked off his feet and dragged, headfirst, across the lawn toward the sidewalk and the street.

11 A Deadly Drag Race

Frank was by the side of the house when he heard shouts from the front yard. One of the voices was a stranger's. The other was Joe's. From the way he was shouting, Joe was obviously in some kind of trouble.

Frank made a dash for the front. As he rounded the corner, he heard the roar of a car engine. Frank tried to make out what was happening in the darkened yard. The car was starting down the driveway toward the street. Something was tied to the truck, bouncing across the lawn after it.

Abruptly the pieces of the puzzle fell into place. Frank froze. He realized that the bundle being dragged behind the car was Joe!

The four-by-four was almost at the street. Someone was crouching in the back, leaning out over the rear-mounted spare tire. Frank could see the pale oval of his face but couldn't identify him.

Frank cut across the lawn on a diagonal, hoping to intercept the car at the street. As he ran, he groped in his jeans pocket for his Swiss Army knife. If he had a second to unfold the main blade and reach the rope, he knew he could save Joe. But the car was already starting to turn onto the street and pick up speed. How would he find the time? It was hopeless!

Gulping for air, Frank put on a new burst of speed and made a flying lunge, managing to close his left hand around the taut rope. With his right he brought the Swiss Army knife up to his mouth and tried to grip the edge of the biggest blade with his front teeth.

His left palm burned as the rough rope slipped through it. Then he tightened his grip and dug his heels into the thick sod. For one moment the line loosened. Then it tightened again, and he, too, was being dragged toward the street.

"Frank!" Joe called, from half a dozen feet behind him. "Let go! You'll get hurt!"

"No way!" Frank gasped. The sidewalk was just ahead. It was now or never. He managed to get the knife blade between his teeth and tugged at the handle to open it. It started to turn.

A moment later his heels skidded off the grass and hit the edge of the concrete sidewalk. He was thrown forward, off-balance. As he flung his weight

94

toward the left, trying to recover, he felt himself lose his grip on the knife. It was jerked out of his hand and teeth and went flying into the darkness.

Frank heard the knife land on the sidewalk. Thinking quickly, he reached over with his now-empty right hand and got a better grip on the rope, then looked ahead.

The four-by-four was just turning onto the street. Its lights were out, and the license plate had been taped over.

Suddenly a car came backing down the driveway across the street. The driver obviously didn't notice the darkened four-by-four pulling out. The four-by-four's tires shrieked as the driver slammed on the brakes. For one instant the rope Frank was holding went slack. In a flash he jumped up and looped it, twice, around the fire hydrant at the curb, then braced himself and hoped.

A moment later the four-by-four swerved around the car that was backing up and started down the street again. Frank counted to himself, "One, two . . ."

The rope jerked tight again, but the friction of the loops against the fire hydrant stopped the rope from slipping. From the four-by-four came a shout of surprise and pain. Joe's assailant must have been holding the rope in his hands. It suddenly went slack, and the vehicle roared off into the night.

Frank ran back to Joe and helped him to his feet, then disentangled the rope from around his arms.

"Are you all right?" he asked breathlessly. "Did you get hurt?"

Joe paused and checked himself over. "That's the fastest I ever wore out a pair of jeans," he reported in a shaken voice. "But luckily my skin is still intact."

Half an hour later Frank and Joe were sitting in their living room, telling their story to Detective Con Riley of the Bayport Police Department. Con was an old friend of theirs, but he still had mixed feelings about taking help from two young detectives who weren't part of any official organization.

"Are you sure the attack is linked to this case you're on now?" he asked when they were finished. "There's more than one crook who wouldn't mind seeing something bad happen to you two."

"That may be," Frank said. "But why attack us now? We know there's already one black four-by-four in the case. We've seen it being driven by two brothers named Eric and Jerry Dresser."

"You're sure the vehicle involved in the attack was black?" Con demanded. "It was pretty dark out there."

"Black, or some very dark color," Joe replied. "The top was down, and it had a heavy-duty roll bar."

"Right," Frank added. "With a row of four or six headlights mounted across the roll bar."

Con Riley closed his notebook and stood up. "I'll put out a call on it. We can retrieve the license number of the Dresser vehicle from Motor Vehicles, but we don't know for sure that that's the one we want. In any case, I doubt if they're still in Bayport."

He looked from Frank to Joe and added, "No vigilante stuff, you guys. You may think you know who was in that car, but finding and punishing them is a matter for the law. Understood?"

"Yes, sir," Frank said.

As soon as they were alone, Joe said, "I plan to have a few words with Eric Dresser."

"Not so fast," Frank said. "You're forgetting his older brother, Jerry, and his gang. This feels more like their work than Eric's."

"What if they're all in it together?" Joe replied. "Eric, his brother, the gang, Devin, and even Karla Newhouse as the brains behind the operation. Doesn't that make sense?"

"As much sense as anything in this case," Frank replied. "Still, at this point, we've got more questions than answers. Who's making the phony Wombats, and where? How do they get them into the Wombat warehouse, so they can be shipped out to stores? And why are they showing up mainly in stores right around here?"

"I think I know the answer to the last question," Joe said. "Stores outside this area are supplied through distributors, but those around here still get their stock directly from the warehouse. That's one more piece of evidence that says the warehouse is involved. But I can't imagine how the counterfeits get into the warehouse. All the stock comes in directly from the factory, right next door. There's no way that . . ."

Joe's voice trailed off. Frank glanced over and saw an astonished look spreading across his brother's face. "What is it?" he demanded.

"I just had a wild, crazy idea," Joe replied. "It can't be, but . . . Sure, it all fits. Listen, Frank. You want to know where the phony Wombats are being made? The same place as the real ones—in the Wombat factory! They get into the warehouse the same way as the real ones, on a forklift truck. I've probably moved some of them over myself!"

Frank stared at his brother for a long moment. Then he slapped his fist in his palm. "I think you've got it!" he exclaimed. "That's why the phonies are such good imitations—they're made with the same materials, on the same machines. The only difference is that the crooks don't take the same kind of care in making them."

A new thought occurred to Frank. "If our idea is right, why don't the crooks put the ultraviolet inspection stamp inside the fakes? If they're using the factory, they must know about it."

"They can't," Joe replied. "Those quality inspectors never let their personal stamps out of their sight. They even take them home at night. Besides, the inspection stamps are dated. Maybe the crooks were afraid that the dates would leave too many clues behind."

Frank rubbed his chin. "Could be," he said. "If the phony shoes are being made in the same factory as the real ones, and then packaged and moved over to the same warehouse, how do the crooks know which are which? While you're at work tomorrow, I'm going to pay another visit to some of the stores that have sold the counterfeit shoes. Between us, we should be able to come up with some more answers."

Outside, a car pulled into the driveway. Frank and Joe stiffened. Was this the start of another attack of some sort?

The front door swung open. Mr. and Mrs. Hardy, along with Aunt Gertrude, came in. Mrs. Hardy looked into the living room and said, "I'll bet you boys are glad you didn't come with us. There's nothing so relaxing as a quiet evening at home, is there?"

Joe gave Frank a conspiratorial glance, then said, "You're so right, Mom."

The next morning Frank dropped Joe off at work, then headed for the mall to pay another visit to Benlow's Sporting Goods.

At the warehouse Joe kept his eyes open, but nothing turned up that seemed to have any bearing on the investigation. He was about to break for lunch when one of the other workers, a guy named Whitney, came over.

"Hey, Hardy," he said. "You play baseball?"

"Sure," Joe replied.

"You ever play second base?"

"Sure," Joe said again. "Why?"

99

"A bunch of us get together during lunch to play, and we're short a second baseman. What do you say?"

"I guess so," Joe said. "What do you do about lunch? I'm going to need to eat, and I didn't bring anything."

"You can buy a sandwich and a drink from the fast-food truck, after the game," Whitney replied. "I've got a spare glove you can use. So, are you on board?"

Joe shrugged. "Sure, why not?" he said.

A few minutes later Joe followed Whitney out to the big vacant lot behind the warehouse and factory. The weeds in the infield had been cut recently, and somebody had laid down squares of linoleum to mark the four bases. Joe noticed that the diamond had been getting a lot of use. The path that circled the bases was worn down to the bare reddish earth.

"Okay, you turkeys, let's play ball!" someone shouted. Joe looked toward the pitcher's mound and saw Linc Metairie tossing a ball up and down. The mitt on his right hand looked as if it had put in a lot of years of service.

Metairie fired the ball toward the plate. It landed with a loud smack in Ray Beane's mitt. "Ow!" Beane cried out. "Hey, Johnnie, take over at catcher, will you? I hurt my hand yesterday."

"Whew! He's fast," Joe said in a low voice.

"That's just warm-ups," Whitney said. "Wait till he really starts cooking. He's accurate, too. Not like some pitchers with speed but nothing else. Let's get to our positions."

Joe moved out to second base. Whitney was playing third. The moment he got there, Metairie shouted, "Heads up, Whitney!" and threw the ball to him, very fast.

The third baseman managed to bring his glove up just in time, stopping the ball. Joe could see him wince with pain from the impact. Then Whitney turned and threw it to Joe.

"Come on, Hardy, throw to first!" the foreman shouted.

Joe paid no attention. He was staring at the baseball in his hand, and at the red dirt ground into the seams of the cover. It looked exactly like a newer version of the one thrown at him and Frank as a warning . . . and now Joe was sure that he knew who had thrown it!

He was dazed by this new light on the case. He threw the ball to first, almost without knowing that he did it. How did Linc's involvement fit with what he and Frank had already learned? If the warehouse foreman was part of the gang of counterfeiters, that meant—

"Joe, watch it!" Whitney's shout broke through Joe's preoccupation. He blinked and then looked around.

Metairie had just launched another fastball. And this one was aimed straight at Joe's head!

12 Some Greasy Footwork

The baseball hurtled toward Joe's head at ninety miles an hour. There was no time to think. Joe dived sideways and hit the dirt. Just in time! He was sure, before he fell, that he felt the ball pass right by his head.

"Come on, Hardy!" Metairie shouted derisively. "We're playing baseball. You're supposed to catch the ball. Not dodge it!"

Joe took a deep breath and pulled himself to his feet. He knew the baseball could have badly hurt or even killed him. From now on, he meant to keep a very close eye on Linc Metairie. If his suspicions were right, his life might just depend on it.

* * *

Frank stood inside the entrance of Benlow's Sporting Goods and looked around. He spotted the tall, burly store owner in the tennis section.

"You again?" Mr. Benlow said as Frank came up to him. "Haven't I answered enough of your questions? What is it this time?"

Frank gave him an innocent smile. "I was wondering if I could look around your stockroom, just to get an idea of how it works," he said.

Mr. Benlow shook his head. He was obviously about to say no when Frank went on.

"Actually, it was Mr. Brinkstead's idea," Frank added quickly. "He said that if I really wanted to learn, I should study your operations."

Mentally Frank crossed his fingers and hoped that Brinkstead would back him up, if Benlow took it into his head to check.

The store owner frowned, as if thinking hard, then said, "Well, okay. But the minute you start getting in our way, out you go."

He picked up the intercom and said, "Eric, one of those guys I told you about the other day is back. He's going to look at our stockroom operations. Don't let him bother you or take your mind off your job. Got it?"

Frank winced. Up until now he and Joe had managed to keep their involvement in the case a secret from Eric. Not anymore. Frank would just have to brave it out.

The intercom squawked. Frank couldn't make out what Eric had said, but he was obviously angry.

"Never mind that," Benlow said. "Just do as I say." He turned to Frank and said, "Go on back."

Frank reached the stockroom door just as Eric opened it. "You!" he said, giving Frank a dirty look. "What are you doing here?"

"I'm studying the store for a class project," Frank replied.

"Huh!" Eric said, pushing past Frank toward the showroom. A moment later Frank was alone in the stockroom. He found the shoe section, then looked around for the Wombats. There were more boxes of them than of any other brand. After looking them over for a couple of minutes, he shrugged in frustration. Except for model and size numbers, every box looked the same, with the same big lettering and stylized picture of a wombat.

Frank pulled out his notebook and checked the numbers he had taken from the Wombat sales computer. He noticed that until two months before, Benlow's generally ordered between 100 and 125 pairs a week. Since then, the orders had dropped off to 60 or less. The most recent one, a week earlier, was for 56 assorted pairs of shoes.

What explained such a huge drop? Maybe sales had slowed, or the store had too much stock. But Frank was betting on another explanation. Benlow's had to be making up the difference with bogus shoes!

At the end of the aisle was a small desk. Frank started toward it, then stopped short. He realized that one of the Wombat boxes he had just passed seemed a little different. But which one, and why?

He took a step back and let his eyes drift along the rows of boxes. Then he laughed to himself. One of the labels had a red blotch in the corner. Big deal—a little spilled ink, that's all.

He was turning to go when he noticed another box, on another shelf, with a red blotch in the same place. He frowned. One might be an accident, but two? Maybe the mark was put there deliberately, to identify certain boxes. He scanned the shelves more carefully and managed to find fourteen more boxes with the mark. Now he was sure that he was on the trail of an important clue.

He decided to check out the desk before Eric or Benlow came back to find out what he was doing. He looked it over, then shrugged in disgust. There was nothing on the desk but some pencils, a tape dispenser, and a rubber date stamp.

Next to the desk was a half-full wastebasket. Frank started sifting through it. None of the crumpled papers seemed important, until he came to a bill from the Wombat Corporation. It documented a shipment of 116 pairs of shoes. He glanced at the date, then sharpened his attention. It was a bill from the previous week. But according to the company computer, that week's order hadn't been 116 pairs of shoes. It had been 56!

He took out his notebook again, to double-check himself, but he'd remembered right. So where had the other sixty pairs of shoes come from? And why had Benlow thrown out the bill? And what were the odds that the labels on their boxes had little red blotches on them?

He folded the bill and put it in his notebook. He was just putting the notebook in his pocket when all the lights in the stockroom went out. Frank whirled around, all his senses alert. This could be a simple power failure, he realized. Or it could be a trap.

To his left, not far away, Frank heard a footstep. He crouched down and turned in that direction with his arms outstretched. Just as his fingers brushed against cloth, something hard crashed down on the left side of his head.

As he recoiled, Frank felt himself slumping to the floor. He fought hard to keep his eyes open, but the dizziness made that impossible.

Hands groped for Frank's arms and jerked them roughly behind his back. He felt a loop of rope tighten on his left wrist. Taking a slow, deep breath, Frank tried to keep his senses alert.

Then, picking the right moment, Frank released all his energy in a slashing attack. His legs swung around, just above floor level, until they connected with something solid. His right fist, still free, delivered a powerful rabbit punch that landed on what he hoped was his opponent's neck.

He heard a sharp intake of breath. The rope around his left wrist loosened. But before he could take advantage of the opportunity, his attacker grabbed his shoulders and slammed his head

106

against the floor. The dizzy feeling returned, stronger than ever, but Frank refused to give in.

He clasped his attacker's wrists and dug his thumbs into the major nerve points, then curled up his legs and lashed out. His feet connected.

His opponent choked out a strangled cry and backed away. As Frank forced himself up into a sitting position, he heard stumbling footsteps in the darkness, then, somewhere at the back of the stockroom, the sound of a slamming door.

Frank's chest heaved as he fought to catch his breath. After a few moments he grabbed the edge of the desk and pulled himself onto his feet. He felt his way through the rows of shelves to the back door and tugged it open.

Outside was one of the mall's service corridors, with plain concrete walls and floors and bright fluorescent lights. Frank blinked at the sudden brightness, then looked in both directions. His attacker was long gone, of course, but just outside the door was a dark puddle where someone had spilled an oily substance. The guy must have stepped in it as he was running away. There was a faint line of footprints on the concrete, leading toward an exit about fifty feet away.

Frank retraced his steps through the stockroom. He brushed off his clothes and reentered the store. No customers were in the store at the moment. Eric was about twenty feet away, folding and shelving a carton of tennis shirts. He glanced up, gave Frank another dirty look, and went on with his work. Mr.

Benlow was at the register near the front of the store, looking at some papers. He, too, glanced up as Frank approached.

"I hope you got what you needed," he said. "We're running a business here, not a school."

"I know," Frank replied. "Thanks for everything."

Without replying, Mr. Benlow went back to his papers.

Frank paused to think. Eric and Mr. Benlow were the only ones who had known that he was in the stockroom. Logically, one of them had to have been his attacker. But which one?

He found the answer sooner than he expected. On the polished floor near the store entrance was a single oily footprint. His attacker must have run around the mall and reentered the store by the main entrance. Frank bent down for a closer look at the footprint. It was clearly from an ordinary shoe. Frank was almost sure that Eric was wearing sneakers, Wombats in fact. He went back into the store to check.

"Left my notebook," he said to Mr. Benlow as he passed. He glanced down. The store owner was wearing brown leather shoes, and there was a faint oily mark on the floor next to him. Frank didn't have to go any farther. Even at that distance, he could see Eric's red, white, and green Wombats.

"Oops, it was in my pocket all the time," he added. He turned and left the store. He could hardly wait to pick up Joe and tell him what he had learned.

Joe got off work at four and walked down the road to the bus stop, where he was to meet Frank. As he walked, he swung his arms forcefully, trying to shake out the tension in his shoulders. He had spent the whole afternoon on guard, convinced that Metairie was going to attack him in some way. The attack never came, but Joe still thought that the foreman was planning something.

Frank pulled up a few moments after Joe reached the bus stop. Joe jumped in, and Frank pulled away.

"I'll tell you my news as we go," Frank said.

"Ditto," Joe said. "By the way, where are we going?"

"Winston Brinkstead should still be in his office," Frank replied. "I think it's time we let him in on what's happening."

As they drove to the Wombat Corporation headquarters, Joe told Frank his discovery of the red clay and of Metairie's pitching skills, then listened to the story of the red blotches on the boxes and the attack on Frank. Frank also filled him in on the differences between what the company computer said about the size of the store's order and what had actually been delivered to the store.

"So Benlow is definitely involved," Joe said when Frank was done. "That makes sense. Someone in authority has to be ordering and paying for the phony shoes, not just a stockroom boy. I still think Eric might be in on the scam, though."

"Let's face it," Frank said with a laugh. "You've got a grudge against him."

Joe rolled his eyes. "Maybe so, but don't forget that someone in a black four-by-four, just like the one he drives, tried to lasso me into the wildest ride of my life yesterday."

"Something about that has been bothering me," Frank said as he pulled into Wombat's parking lot. "I want another look at that four-by-four."

Within a few minutes Frank and Joe were inside Brinkstead's office. "I was meaning to call you fellows," Winston said when they walked in. "I'm very eager to know if you've made any progress and if there's any way I can be of more help."

"I think we're getting somewhere," Joe replied. "First of all, we're pretty sure the phony shoes are being shipped from your own warehouse, and that the foreman, Linc Metairie, is involved." He and Frank had agreed before going to headquarters not to mention their theory that the counterfeits were being produced in the Wombat factory. At this point the evidence for that was just too weak.

"I can't believe it," Brinkstead said when Joe finished. "I've known Linc for ten years."

"We've also established that the owner of Benlow's Sporting Goods is in on the scheme," Frank said. "Last week, for example, his shipment of Wombats contained sixty more pairs of shoes than were listed on the order in the computer. And a number of the boxes had the same red mark on the label. We're betting that they contain the counterfeits."

"Oh, and don't forget Devin Porter," Joe said. When Brinkstead looked blank, he added, "Devin's the stock clerk at the factory outlet. He has a bad reputation and some very suspicious friends. It seems likely that he's involved."

Mr. Brinkstead shook his head from side to side. "Unbelievable," he said. "Simply unbelievable."

Joe turned his head sharply. He heard a distinct noise outside the office door. He sprang up and opened it. Karla Newhouse was standing there. Her hand was in the air, ready to knock. When she saw Joe, she took a step backward.

"Sorry, Win," she said, looking past Joe. She sounded breathless. "Can I talk to you? It's about the reorganization plan."

Mr. Brinkstead said, "Sure, Karla. Will you fellows excuse me for a moment? No, no, stay where you are. I'll just step outside."

While he was gone, Joe glanced at the papers on his desk. One had big red exclamation marks scrawled next to a paragraph. It concerned a plan to cut the national sales department and give its responsibilities to the marketing division. Joe was about to ask Frank if he remembered Brinkstead's title when the door opened.

"I'm sorry, fellows," Mr. Brinkstead said.

111

"Something's come up that we have to deal with right away. We'll have to meet again in a day or two, if that's okay."

"Sure," Frank said, getting to his feet. "We understand."

Downstairs, he turned to Joe and said, "How long do you think Karla Newhouse was outside that door? Long enough to hear our report?"

Joe frowned. "I'd assume so."

"Can you sneak us into the warehouse?" Frank asked. "I want to look for any boxes with red marks before the gang has time to hide them."

Joe made a face. "I think so," he said. "We'd better be pretty careful, though. If we get caught, I'll lose my job."

Frank laughed and they piled back in the van. They drove to the industrial park and left the van down the road from the Wombat warehouse. Joe led the way around the back of the building to the loading dock. He and Frank hid behind a trailer until the guard was distracted by an approaching forklift. Then they dashed through the entrance.

"The warehouse staff is on staggered shifts," Joe explained in a low voice, once they were inside. "By now, there shouldn't be more than one or two guys around. The outgoing shipments are over here, near the dispatcher's office."

The dispatcher's office was a cubicle with partitions that were thin metal up to waist level and glass the rest of the way up. Next to it were several wooden pallets stacked high with cardboard cartons. Joe scanned the shipping labels until he found one addressed to a store near Bayport. Then he and Frank looked over the cartons, keeping a lookout for anyone who might spot them.

"Here!" Frank exclaimed, pointing to a carton near the bottom of the stack. "See that red mark?"

Joe was bending down to look when he heard footsteps nearby. He grabbed Frank's arm and pulled him behind one of the stacks of cartons. A moment later Ray Beane came into view. As he walked, he pulled off his leather work gloves. His left hand had a wide bandage across the palm. He went into the office, leaving the door open, and made a phone call.

"We're all set," Joe heard him say. "Yeah, it's tonight."

After a pause Beane added, "I understand. No, I don't know how they caught on. But they'd better not get in our way. If they do, we'll take care of them—permanently!"

13 The Stakes Get Raised

Frank sucked in his breath and motioned for Joe to be quiet. Beane hung up the phone, and there was silence for a few moments, then the sound of tearing paper. Frank raised himself from his crouched position behind the booth and risked a peek through the glass part of the partition. Beane had a thick file folder open on the table in front of him. He took some papers from it and tore them into small pieces, which he dropped into a paper bag.

Frank ducked his head down and looked around. The opening to one of the aisles was just a few feet away. He touched Joe's arm, pointed to the aisle, and raised his eyebrows questioningly. Joe paused for a moment, then nodded.

114

Frank took another quick glance through the window. Beane had his back to them and was still busy destroying papers. Frank scurried to the shelter of the nearby aisle. Joe was right behind.

The aisle was empty. Joe pointed toward the far end, then set off between the tall stacks of cartons. Frank followed him.

At the end of the aisle Joe took Frank's arm and brought his mouth close to Frank's ear. "This way," he whispered. "Follow me."

He walked around the corner, whistling softly. About fifty feet away was a time clock and a rack of cards. A guard was sitting on a high stool next to an open doorway, looking at a magazine.

The guard glanced up at Joe and Frank for a moment, then looked back at his magazine. Joe took a card from the rack, punched it, and put it back. Frank did the same. As they made for the door, Joe said, "See you."

"Yeah, see ya," the guard replied without looking up.

As they walked quickly across the parking lot, Frank took a deep breath. "That took a lot of nerve," he said. "What if he'd stopped us?"

Joe grinned. "Why should he? His job is to keep people out, not keep people in. Once he saw my face and remembered me, that was it. And he probably didn't bother to look at you at all."

Back in the van Joe said, "Now we're getting somewhere. We know that Beane is part of the gang, along with Metairie. We know that something

115

important is going to happen tonight. We should come back later and stake out the place."

Frank drummed his fingers on the steering wheel. "Sure," he said. "Good idea. But who was Beane talking to? That's what I'd like to know."

"Metairie?" Joe suggested.

Frank thought that over. "I don't know," he said slowly. "Whoever it was warned Beane that we were on to them. Who's in a position to know that? Aside from Winston Brinkstead, there's Karla Newhouse and Benlow."

"We know Benlow is part of it," Joe pointed out. "Don't forget Eric and his brother. Not to mention Devin, who has some kind of relationship with Eric's brother *and* Karla Newhouse."

Frank felt as if his head was spinning. "We've got too many suspects!" he exclaimed. "It's time to start eliminating some of them."

"Great idea," Joe replied. "But how?"

As he turned the ignition key, Frank said, "We ask some questions and see what we get in the way of answers. Let's start with Eric. He should be off work by now. I hope there aren't too many Dressers in the Holman Heights phone book."

It turned out there was only one Dresser in Holman Heights. Frank got the address by calling information from the cellular phone in the van. The Hardys quickly drove to the address listed. It turned out to be one of a row of two-story brick houses a couple of blocks from the pizzeria Frank had been to the day before.

116

An older woman answered the door. When Joe told her they wanted to see Eric, she turned to the staircase and called, "Eric? Some friends of yours to see you."

Eric hurried down the stairs, then stopped short as he recognized Frank and Joe.

"Okay, Mom," he said in a taut voice. "I'll take care of this."

His mother looked at him with concern. Then she went into the living room and closed the door.

"What do you guys want?" Eric demanded, his hands jammed into his pockets.

"We just want to ask a few questions," Frank replied. "Mostly about Wombat shoes. I notice you're wearing some right now——"

Eric held up his hand. "I'll be back in a minute," he said. "I'm in the middle of a phone call." With that, he turned and walked toward the back of the house.

Frank met Joe's eyes and shrugged. After a short pause he said, "I don't hear Eric's voice. Do you?"

As if in answer, a door slammed.

"He took off out the back door," Frank said urgently. "Come on!"

The living room door opened, and Eric's mother peered out, a worried look on her face.

"Thanks," Frank said as he pulled open the front door. "We have to go now."

Out on the sidewalk Frank and Joe looked in both directions. There were no yards between any of the houses on the block. How could Eric hope to get away from them?

"There must be an alley behind the houses," Joe said. He set off at a run for the nearest corner. Frank followed him. Just as they reached the corner, they heard a squeal of tires. A second later a black four-by-four shot out of the alley and made a wide turn onto the side street. As it flashed by, Joe caught a glimpse of Eric's face. He looked frightened. The car turned the corner and disappeared.

"That clinches it," Joe said. "He's part of the gang, and now he's running off to warn the others."

Frank didn't answer. He was still looking down the street.

"What is it?" Joe demanded. "What's wrong?"

"The headlights," Frank replied. "Of course! There weren't any headlights on the roll bar."

"What?" Joe said. "What do you mean?"

"That isn't the car we saw last night, the one that tried to drag you off," Frank went on. "Don't you remember? It had at least four headlights mounted on the roll bar. We told Con Riley about them. But Eric's car doesn't have any."

Joe was silent for a few moments. Then he said, "Maybe he took them off."

Frank shook his head. "No way. Now that I think of it, his car didn't have those headlights the day of the track meet, when we saw it the first time. Or when I saw his brother with it at the outlet a couple of days ago. There must be another black four-by-

118

four in this case. And its driver is the same person who tried to drag you."

"If Eric's innocent, why did he run away?" Joe asked.

"I don't know," Frank admitted. "But we do know his older brother is involved in *something* shady, and we know that it has something to do with Devin Porter. Maybe Devin has some answers."

Five minutes later Frank and Joe were climbing the outside staircase of the three-story building where Devin lived. At the open landing on the second floor, Joe paused and looked out over the railing at the street below. Thirty feet down, Joe could see the cars passing by on the street out front.

They continued up the stairs to the top floor. Yellow light came through from the windows on either side of the door. A card was thumbtacked just below the doorbell. Joe leaned close and read Newhouse-Porter.

He pressed the button and heard a buzz inside. Footsteps approached, and the door swung open. The person was silhouetted against the lights of the room, but after an instant, Joe recognized Karla Newhouse.

In that same moment she must have recognized him and Frank. "You!" she choked out. "What are you doing here? How dare you follow me."

Joe was opening his mouth to answer her when a hand pushed her to one side.

"I knew you guys wouldn't leave me alone," a

voice said. Joe saw it was Devin. The boy's voice rose to a shout. "I knew you'd keep picking on me. But I'm not going to take any more of it!"

He came charging out the door at the two Hardys. Frank managed to sidestep him, but Joe felt himself grabbed around the waist and forced back across the open landing.

Joe's back slammed against the wooden railing, and he felt Devin pushing him backward. He took a quick glance over his shoulder. It was a long drop. He grasped Devin's shoulders and tried to push him away. Then, to his horror, Joe heard the sound of splintering wood and felt the railing start to bend outward. In another second they were both going to plunge thirty feet to the sidewalk!

14 A Big Breakthrough

"Joe! Hold on!"

Frank made a wild leap across the landing. He grabbed Devin's collar and reached his other hand out to pull at Joe's sleeve. Grimly Frank braced his feet against the railing's supports. He kept his grip on Devin and Joe. Finally they broke their momentum and came falling back toward Frank.

Devin went flying and crashed into the wall, right next to the door. Joe fell on top of Frank.

"Oof," Frank said as Joe's elbow dug into the pit of his stomach. "Try landing somewhere else next time!"

"Sorry," Joe replied. "But you looked a lot softer than the sidewalk down there."

They scrambled to their feet, ready to go after

121

Devin. But he was still slumped against the wall with a dazed expression on his face.

Karla Newhouse and another woman with shoulder-length dark hair, who looked a lot like Karla, rushed over and knelt down next to Devin.

Karla looked up at Frank and said accusingly, "You didn't have to be so rough with him."

Frank's jaw fell. After a few seconds he managed to say, "I'm sorry, but he almost killed my brother. Not to mention himself."

"He's right, Karla," the second woman said. "They would have both gone over the edge if this guy hadn't stopped them."

She turned back to Devin and said, "Take a deep breath and try to calm down. Whatever happens, we'll back you up. You know that."

"I'm sorry," Devin said in an exhausted voice. "Every time I turn around, somebody else is on my case. I just couldn't take any more."

"I understand," the woman replied. She looked at Frank and Joe again. "Let's go inside. I'd rather not have the whole neighborhood hear our problems."

She and Karla helped Devin to his feet. Frank and Joe followed them into the living room. Devin slumped onto the sofa. Karla turned off the TV and sat down next to him.

"Have a seat," the other woman said, waving her hand in the direction of two easy chairs. "I'd better introduce myself. I'm Donna Newhouse-Porter, Devin's mother."

122

"She's also my sister," Karla added. "As you've probably figured out by now."

"Yes," Frank said, nodding. "We worked that out from the names. What I don't know is why Devin attacked us just now."

"He's been under a lot of pressure—" Donna started to say.

Karla cut her off. "I think we should be frank," she said. "Last year Devin got into trouble with the police. It wasn't his fault. He was running around with the wrong crowd, that's all, but he was the one who paid the price."

"Are we talking about Jerry Dresser and his friends?" Frank asked.

Karla's eyes widened. "You *are* a detective," she said. "Yes, Jerry and his gang. Anyway, Devin needed a chance to prove he'd straightened himself out. I pulled a few strings and got him a job at the Wombat factory outlet. He was doing fine until the other day, when his so-called friends found out where he was working and paid him a visit."

"The same day we came by?" Frank asked.

Devin shook his head. "No, a week or two before," he said. "The day you were there, they were just giving me a little reminder. They jumped you to put more pressure on me."

"What did they want?" Joe asked.

"Shoes, what else?" Devin replied. "Without paying for them. They wanted me to sneak Wombats out of the store. They were going to sell them and make a lot of bread. They said if I didn't do it,

123

they'd send a letter to the company, telling them about my record and claiming I stole from the store."

"You were really in a bind, weren't you?" Frank said sympathetically. "What did you do?"

"I stalled them," Devin said. "I tried to think of a way out. I knew if my past got out, nobody would believe me. Once you've been in trouble, people are always ready to think the worst."

He took a deep breath before adding, "Then you guys started snooping around. I was sure you'd find out about me and tell the company. I was right— you *did* find out."

Frank glanced over at Joe, who just shrugged in confusion. "What, exactly, did we find out?" Frank asked, looking amused.

Devin stared at him. "Why, about Aunt Karla, of course," he said. "I couldn't let her lose her job because she'd done me a good turn, could I?"

Karla put her arm around Devin's shoulders and gave him a squeeze. "What Devin is trying to say," she told Joe and Frank, "is that Wombat has a strict policy about hiring relatives. I broke that when I got Devin his job at the factory outlet."

"Is hiring a stock clerk such a big deal?" Joe asked.

"Yes and no," Karla said with a shrug. "Ordinarily it probably wouldn't matter if it got out. Except that I was brought in by the new management that took over this year—and that made some old-timers resentful. On top of that the new team is hard-nosed. They're trimming jobs and getting rid of old-timers on every side. There's even talk about eliminating whole departments."

Joe remembered the memo he had seen on Winston's desk. National sales was one of those departments. He didn't say anything, though. If he asked Karla, he'd have to admit he was snooping on Winston's desk.

Karla sighed. "The point is, there are people in the company who would love to get something on me, something they could use to get me fired."

"Is that why you didn't want us investigating?" Joe asked. "Because you thought we might find out about Devin?"

"Of course," Karla said, giving him a puzzled look. "What other reason could there be?"

"What about the counterfeit shoes?" Frank asked.

"What about them?" Karla replied. "Sure, it's a problem—a *big* problem. But once we find out the source of the shoddy imitations and shut it down, our customers will come back. They know that Wombat has always stood for quality."

Frank studied Karla's face. Unless he was wrong, she looked completely innocent. Still, *someone* had been keeping the gang informed of every move that he and Joe made.

"When you arranged for Joe to work at the warehouse," Frank pursued, "did you tell anyone

—anyone at all—who he was and what he was doing there?"

Karla blinked a couple of times before saying, "No, of course not. I had to tell personnel that it was something out of the ordinary, but I certainly didn't say what. Why do you ask?"

Joe cut in. "Ten minutes after I started work the other day, somebody tried to dump a few hundred pounds of cartons on my head," he said. "I think someone was tipped off that I was coming."

"I can't imagine how—" Karla began. She fell silent for a few moments, then said, "You think I'm part of the counterfeiting racket, don't you?"

"The thought crossed our minds," Frank admitted.

Karla looked from him to Joe, then back again. "That is so ridiculous, I don't know what to say. Or no, it's not actually ridiculous. I guess I'd be well placed to do something like that. But I didn't. I wouldn't. Even if they fire me, I wouldn't lower myself. I couldn't sleep nights, knowing that I had done something dishonest."

Frank sneaked a glance at his watch. It was a few minutes after eight. The last of the staggered shifts at the Wombat factory and warehouse must have gotten off work. It was time for him and Joe to get over there and set up their stakeout.

"Look," he said to Karla. "We're probably going to have to ask you some more questions. For now, though, we won't say anything about Devin."

"Oh, thank you!" Devin's mother exclaimed.

126

Both Devin and Karla looked torn between doubt and relief. Frank wondered why. Were they simply relieved that he and Joe weren't going to blow the whistle on them? Or that they had managed to keep them from uncovering a more important secret?

On the way across town the Hardys paused at a drive-in restaurant to stock up on some sandwiches and coffee. Once they got to the industrial park, Joe cruised around until he found a spot between two parked trailers that was hidden but had a good view of the Wombat factory gate.

Joe settled back in his seat, unwrapped a turkey sandwich, and kept his eyes peeled on the factory.

An hour passed, then another. Except for a floodlight over the entrance, the Wombat factory stayed dark. Joe suppressed a yawn, then almost cracked his jaw when a bigger yawn came along. He reached over to the console between the two front seats and took a sip from a can of soda.

"Frank?" he said. "I know Ray said that tonight was the night. But he didn't say where. Maybe the gang is meeting someplace else."

"Maybe," Frank said. He sounded tired. "But this is the only lead we have. Let's give it three or four more hours. If nothing turns up, we can go home and start over again tomorrow."

Joe took a deep breath. Three or four hours? He didn't think he could last that long. "You mind if I take a nap?" he asked.

"I wouldn't do that if I were you," Frank said, in an urgent tone. He leaned forward. "Look."

A dark-colored four-by-four with a row of headlights on the roll bar had just stopped outside the Wombat gate.

"That's the one!" Frank exclaimed. "So now we *know* that it wasn't Eric and Jerry Dresser's car we saw last night."

The nightwatchman came out and flashed his light on the guys in the car. Joe counted four of them.

"I can't see the faces of the others, but that's Ray Beane in the back seat," Joe said as the gate swung open. "I bet he's the one who lassoed me. That's why he had a bandage on his hand today. He must have gotten a bad rope burn."

The four-by-four pulled up near the factory door, and the four men went inside. The guard went inside, too, leaving the front gate open slightly.

"Come on!" Joe reached for the door handle. "Before he remembers to come back and close it!"

He and Frank ran silently to the gate, slipped through, and ran across the parking lot to the factory entrance. Inside, the huge space was silent and empty. Strange shapes loomed up in the dim light. Suddenly, twenty yards away, a row of bright work lights came on. Joe shut his eyes briefly against the glare. Moments later he heard the whirr of machinery. Someone had just started one of the factory's automated production lines.

"Okay, this is it," Ray Beane's voice said from somewhere nearby. The voice startled Joe, and he crouched lower, behind another machine. Frank did the same.

"Nothing but Hexacell Champs tonight," Ray continued. "Then we wrap it up and divide the quarter of a million. By this time tomorrow I'm planning to be lying on a beach in the Caribbean!"

"Not me," a gruff voice replied. "I'm going to be shopping for a sports car."

Joe risked a peek. Ray was talking to the burly guy who had given Joe directions in the factory the day before. A third guy was standing at a control panel with his back to the first two. That left one person still unaccounted for.

"You know," the burly guy added, "it's a shame to have to give up a sweet deal like this after just two months. I wish I could lay my hands on those kids who blew it for us."

"No problem, Stu," a loud voice announced. "They're right here!"

Joe leapt to his feet and spun around. Linc Metairie was standing a few feet away, a wicked smile on his face. Instantly Joe charged at the warehouse foreman, pushing him against one of the machines. Before Metairie could recover, Joe dodged to the left and began sprinting down the aisle toward the door. Frank was right behind him.

Suddenly Frank's footsteps stopped, and Joe heard a strangled cry for help. He spun on his heel

129

and looked back. Metairie had grabbed Frank and thrown him against a machine that stitched the leather tops of the athletic shoes. The sleeve of Frank's jacket was tangled in the conveyor belt. The machine's powerful needles were whizzing up and down, only inches from Frank's face!

15 Stitched and Tied

For one terrible moment Frank stared at the needles of the stitching machine, almost hypnotized by the gleam of light on their fast-moving shafts.

Then he made a convulsive movement, trying to wrench himself free. It was no use. His jacket was firmly caught in a pair of metal jaws that carried the shoes along the production line. Step by deadly step it was pulling him, shoulder first, toward the razor-sharp needles.

Frank twisted his head to one side and shouted, "Joe! Run for it!"

Frank's left hand was still free. He reached up and unzipped his jacket, then pulled to the left, trying to free his right arm. He gained a few inches, but the conveyor belt had drawn the sleeve so tightly around his upper arm that he couldn't pull it loose.

There were angry shouts somewhere close by. Someone tripped over his legs, then gave him a painful kick in the shin. Before he knew what was happening, Frank felt powerful arms wrap around his waist. He was being tugged away from the machine.

"Hold on," Joe's voice shouted, close to his ear. "I see the switch!"

The tug at his waist grew stronger for a moment, then disappeared. He heard Joe shout, "Out of my way," then the sound of a fist making contact.

"Unnh!" a different voice said.

An instant later the stitching machine stopped and the metal jaws released. There were a few seconds of silence, then Metairie shouted, "Stu, Ray! Grab them! Quick!"

Frank pulled his jacket free and spun around. A few feet away Joe was grappling with two guys. Frank launched himself in their direction. At that moment Joe managed to trip one of the guys, who fell backward, right into Frank's path. Frank stumbled and collided with a metal hand truck, giving himself a solid crack on the forehead.

In a daze, Frank felt rough hands grab his arms and tie them behind his back. He pulled his knees up and tried to kick out at his captors, but they grabbed his legs and tied them at the ankles. Then he was dragged across the floor and into an open space in the middle of the factory. With a sinking feeling Frank realized he didn't have his pocket knife with him. He wouldn't be able to cut his way out of his binding.

A moment later Joe was dropped next to him. His arms and legs were tied, too.

Metairie grabbed a handful of Frank's jacket and pulled him up into a sitting position. "You boys don't look so smart now," he sneered.

"You can't keep us here, you know," Frank said. He forced himself to speak as calmly and confidently as possible. "We spoke to a high official of the Wombat Corporation this afternoon and told him everything we've found out."

Next to him Joe pulled himself into a sitting position and said, "That's right. And Con Riley of the Bayport police knows where all our notes are."

For a moment the foreman's face turned into that of an enraged animal. Frank flinched as Metairie pulled back his fist, ready to smash it into Frank's jaw. But the blow didn't come.

"Aw, why bust my hand on you?" Metairie said. He took a step backward. "You don't matter anymore. By the time anyone finds you, we'll be long gone, living it up."

"This was quite a racket you dreamed up," Joe said, with a hint of admiration in his voice. "You must have made a pile out of it."

Frank understood what Joe was doing. The longer they kept Metairie talking, the better their chances for finding a way out of the situation.

"You're telling me," Metairie replied. "We've been shipping over a thousand units a week for the past eight weeks, and it's all gravy."

For a moment Frank was confused. Over a thousand a week? Hadn't Karla's memo mentioned fewer than that? Then he understood. Karla had been talking about the defective counterfeits that came back to the company. Metairie was talking about how many pairs they actually sent out to stores.

"What about materials?" Joe asked. "Won't the shortages be noticed?"

"Sure, one of these days," Metairie said. "For now the computer says everything is fine. It ought to. That's what Ray told it to say."

Frank did some quick calculations in his head. A thousand pairs of phony Wombats a week, times eight weeks, times fifty bucks a pair, came to four hundred thousand dollars!

"Why are you guys only dividing a quarter of a million?" Frank asked. "Where's the other hundred and fifty thousand going?"

Metairie gave him a cold look and didn't answer. Frank got the feeling the other three members of the gang were listening.

"It can't be overhead," Frank continued. "You already said you don't have any. There must be someone taking a cut off the top. That seems unfair. You guys do all the work, and someone else ends up with the biggest share of the money."

"Shut up!" Metairie shouted. He kicked Frank in

the side, then started to walk away. "We don't have time to listen to this garbage. We've got work to do. Ray, if either of these clowns lets out another peep, cram a rag down his throat!"

Frank looked over at Joe and gave a tiny shake of his head. It wasn't worth pushing Metairie any further at this point. Their best strategy was to watch for a chance to turn the tables on the gang.

Stu, the nearest guy, was twenty feet away, watching over one of the machines. Ray was with him, his back to Frank and Joe. Metairie was gone.

"Listen," Frank whispered to Joe. "How good a job did they do of tying you up?"

After a moment Joe said, "It feels pretty solid."

"If you can get your wrists close to my hands," Frank said, "I'll work on the knots."

Another silence, then faint scuffling sounds. Frank felt Joe's shoulder bump into his arm. He groped around behind his back and found his brother's bound wrists.

"It feels like they used quarter-inch nylon," Frank whispered. "That's good. Synthetics don't hold knots as well as hemp."

"The guy who had tied me up obviously believed in quantity instead of quality," Joe whispered back. "I swear he wrapped my wrists half a dozen times before tying the knots."

Frank began to tug at the outermost knot. By the time it began to loosen, his fingertips felt raw and sore. Luckily, the next knot was easier, and the one after that practically untied itself.

135

"Joe?" Frank whispered. "I'm tucking the ends between your arms so the rope still looks tied."

"Check," Joe muttered back. "Let me start on you now."

"Hey!" Stu suddenly shouted. "Those guys are up to some funny business!"

He ran over to Frank, grabbed him under the arms, and dragged him out of Joe's reach. Frank's heart sank. Once Stu got a look at Joe's ropes, he would see that they had been untied. He and Joe had just lost their best chance to escape.

Stu gave the rope on Frank's arms a painful jerk, then went back to Joe. He was bending over to check the rope on Joe's wrists when a bell started ringing at the control station.

"Now what!" Stu growled as he hurried away.

Frank was about to motion for Joe to make a move when Metairie appeared around the corner. He gave Frank a mean look, squatted down, and started searching Frank's pockets. Metairie found the van's registration in Frank's wallet and the spare set of keys in his jacket pocket.

"Ray?" he called out. The dispatcher came over.

"Go find their van and bring it around to the loading dock," Metairie continued. "These boys are dying to go for a ride."

"Listen, Linc," Ray said, chewing on the end of his mustache. "Why don't we just lock them in a storeroom or something while we make our getaway? You never said anything about—"

"Getting cold feet, Ray?" Metairie replied. He

136

gave the dispatcher a hard look. "I seem to remember you didn't mind trying to push a few hundred pounds of cartons onto Junior's head or dragging him down the street behind Wally's car."

Ray shook his head. "I only meant to scare them, you know that. The same with that dye you put in their drinks. You told me yourself that it wouldn't do more than make them sick."

"That was then," Metairie said. "This is now. You do as you're told, or you can whistle for your share of the quarter-million. Go find that van."

Ray hesitated for another moment, then took the keys and left. Once he was out of the building, Metairie turned to the fourth gang member, a burly bald guy with a square jaw.

"Wally?" the foreman said. "I'm going to borrow your four-by-four. Ray can drive it. I'll take the van. I don't trust Ray alone with these kids. You know the pond out on Route forty-six?"

"Sure," Wally responded. "I used to swim there when I was a kid. They say it's at least fifty feet deep."

"Right," Metairie said. "If I leave the windows of the van open, it should sink out of sight and never be found. Oh—and don't be surprised if I come back without Ray. Guys who get cold feet at a time like this are too much of a danger to the rest of us."

"Yeah, I'm with you there," Wally growled. "I wouldn't mind getting his share, either."

Frank's blood ran cold at this exchange. He and Joe had faced deadly danger many times, but the thought of waiting, trapped and helpless, as the van sank into the icy waters of the pond brought a chilly sweat to his forehead. He took a deep breath and tried to break the cord twisted around his wrists. The blood roared in his ears, and the numbness in his hands gave way to piercing pain, but it was no use. The cord was much too strong.

They had only one hope—that no one would discover Joe's loosened knots.

"Okay, Linc," Ray called a few minutes later. "The van's out back."

Metairie grabbed Frank and dragged him toward the loading dock. After a short distance he said, "Ray, take this guy's feet. Wally, you and Stu bring the other one."

At the van Metairie dumped Frank on the floor in the back. A moment later Joe's body landed on top of him. The door slammed, the engine roared, and the van started off with a jerk. As it made a sharp turn out of the parking lot, Joe rolled off his brother. Frank felt Joe's fingers begin to tug at the rope around his wrists.

After a few minutes Joe leaned his head close to Frank's ear. "The knots won't budge," he whispered.

Metairie, at the wheel, had sharp ears. "You guys shut up back there," he warned. "Or I'll take care of you here and now."

Joe silently continued to work on Frank's knots. Frank lay still and tried to think of a way out. What was Metairie planning? If the villain took the time

138

to put him and Joe into the front seats, to make the drowning look like an accident, they might be able to find an opening. But what if he just kept them in the back and pushed the van into the pond? They'd be trapped for sure!

Ten minutes later the van slowed down and turned off the highway onto a dirt road. Frank's wrists were still firmly tied. He twisted around until he was facing the van's side door. He drew up his knees against his chest, ready to kick out.

Whatever happened in the next few minutes, he was not about to go quietly.

16 Sewing Up
the Case

As the van turned off the highway, Joe gave up trying to untie Frank's hands. The knots were too tight.

"I'm going to have to go it alone," he whispered to his brother.

Frank nodded helplessly. Joe quickly shook the rope off his wrists and reached down to work on the knots at his ankles. When they took another turn, Joe felt his shoulder bump against the van's tool chest.

"Frank," Joe whispered, indicating the tool chest with his head.

Frank's eyes went wide. He bit his lower lip and tipped his head, urging Joe to go ahead.

Feverishly Joe unlatched the lid and scrabbled

around inside. After a moment his hand closed on a screwdriver. He pulled it out and forced the point of the blade into the tightest of the knots. He twisted and pried until he felt the knot start to loosen. Then he dropped the screwdriver and worked at the knot with his fingers. He was just pulling the end of the rope free when the van bumped to a stop. The four-by-four's headlights shone through the van's rear window for a moment, then went dark.

Metairie climbed out and slammed the door. Joe quickly wrapped the rope around Frank's wrist. A moment later the van's side door slid open. Frank and Joe saw the man's form dimly in the dark night.

"Take a look at them," Metairie said. "Make sure they're all right."

"What do you mean, all right?" Ray said. "They're tied up. How's anybody supposed to believe they were in an accident?"

"I'll take care of that in a minute," Metairie replied. "But first—"

Joe's stomach lurched as he recognized the thud of a club landing against the side of a head. Ray gave a sort of sigh and slumped across Joe's legs, then slid to the ground.

Joe peered at the open door. Silhouetted against the sky, Metairie loomed like a giant. He climbed inside and shone a faint light at Frank's wrists, which still looked as if they were bound tightly. Then he turned and bent over Joe.

Joe didn't waste a second. He put every bit of

141

energy he had into clapping his open palms over Metairie's ears, then followed with a forearm to the throat. Metairie lunged at him. At that instant Frank kicked out and caught him in the chest. Metairie sprang up, banged his head on the ceiling of the van, and stumbled backward through the doorway. A moment later Joe heard a scream, followed by a splash.

"He fell into the pond," Frank said urgently. "Quick, cut these ropes on my ankles. We have to rescue him."

Joe found the switch for the ceiling light, then untied Frank. Moments later they were standing on the edge of a cliff overlooking the pond. Joe shone a powerful flashlight down into the pond. The surface of the water was at least twenty feet below them. Could Metairie have remained conscious after such a fall?

"Over there!" Frank exclaimed, pointing to the left. "Isn't that him, on that dock?"

Joe focused the light on the wooden dock and saw what looked like a bundle of wet laundry. Then it moved a little, and he realized that Frank was right. Metairie had managed to swim to the side and climb onto the dock before collapsing.

"Come on," Joe said. "I'll climb down and bring him up. Oh, and we'd better tie up Ray, just in case. Thanks to Metairie and his gang, we've got plenty of rope for the job."

Bringing the unconscious gang leader up from the ledge to the top of the cliff was an exhausting job, but finally Frank and Joe got it done. They put Metairie in the back of the van, next to Ray. Then Joe looked at his watch.

"Almost three A.M.," he reported. As he reached for the van's cellular phone, he gave Frank a grin. "Do you think Con Riley will kill me for waking him up at this hour?"

The Bayport police officer picked up on the second ring.

"We're out of your jurisdiction," Joe said after identifying himself. "But if you know anyone on the force in Holman Heights, you should both meet us at the Wombat factory as soon as possible. Oh, and bring some backup. The guys we're dealing with might put up a fight."

"Do you remember that Marx Brothers movie we saw a while back?" Joe asked in a low voice. "The scene where everybody ended up in one small room?"

Frank glanced around the warehouse office. It was almost eight A.M., and the Holman Heights Police Department had spent the last two hours rounding up all the suspects and witnesses.

"I see what you mean," Frank replied, suppressing a yawn that turned into a grin.

Winston Brinkstead and Karla Newhouse were standing together near the window. Devin Porter was hanging out near Karla and darting nervous glances at Detective Con Riley and his friend, Sergeant Velma Prince of the Holman Heights

143

Police Department. In the far corner Ray Beane, his eyes closed, his head bandaged, and his wrists in handcuffs, was slumped on a chair next to a uniformed police officer.

The door opened. Another officer walked in, his hand resting lightly on Eric Dresser's elbow. Eric's face reddened when he spotted Joe and Frank.

"I knew you guys were pure grief," he said loudly. "But you can't pin anything on me. I haven't done a thing."

"Then you don't have anything to worry about," Frank replied in a good-natured voice. "And thanks for coming, by the way."

"Did I have a choice?" Eric replied bitterly. He glanced at the officer next to him.

The door swung open again. Frank looked around and said, "Well! And here's our guest of honor!"

Lincoln Metairie was standing in the doorway. His arms were handcuffed behind his back. When his eyes met Frank's, the look he gave him was pure venom. Metairie took a menacing step forward. From behind, two police officers grabbed his arms.

"I don't understand," Karla Newhouse said, turning to Frank and Joe. "You mean one of our own people was behind the counterfeiting scheme?"

"That's right," Joe replied. "Not only that, the gang was making the phony Wombats right here at the Wombat factory, with materials they stole from the company. They'd ship them out to stores along with the real shoes."

144

"That's pretty amazing," Con Riley said. "I'm surprised anyone even knew they were phonies."

"A lot of people who bought them didn't know," Frank observed. "And still don't. As near as I can figure, about half of the counterfeits didn't turn out to be defective. If the gang had been just a little more careful in manufacturing them, they probably would have gotten away with it for a long time. That's one of the weird things about this case."

Joe took up the story. "Another strange thing is that the crooks weren't nearly greedy enough. Sure, they made almost half a million dollars in two months, just passing the phonies on the East Coast. But they could have made millions more by going national. Why didn't they even think of it?"

"Well?" Devin asked, an intent look on his face. "Why didn't they?"

"For one thing," Joe replied, "they needed the cooperation of crooked store owners."

"Hey," Eric said. "You mean guys like Benlow? I *knew* there was something shady about that guy."

"That's right," Frank said. "Mr. Benlow is one of the people who are going to have some explaining to do to the police."

The corners of Eric's mouth turned up into a satisfied smile. "Good. I never liked the guy."

"There are also other store owners who will have to be apprehended," Frank said.

"Right," Con said. "What else, Joe?"

Velma Prince was taking furious notes as Joe and

145

Frank told the story. She nodded, urging Joe to continue.

"Having to deal directly with the store owners made it hard for the crooks to expand beyond this area," Joe explained. "They didn't even try. In fact, the way they ran their operation makes it seem as though they weren't in it for the money at all."

"*I* was," Ray Beane said suddenly. "I admit it. I saw a chance, and like an idiot, I grabbed it." He shook his head sadly, glancing down at his handcuffs. "Like an idiot," he repeated.

Karla gave him a sympathetic glance. Then she said, "Metairie, I find it hard to believe you dreamed up such a complicated scheme. You were well placed to take care of making and shipping the imitation Wombats. But what about the rest? Finding and dealing with store owners? Collecting and handling large sums of money? Organizing and keeping the whole operation running smoothly? That calls for a high level of executive ability. You were really wasted as a warehouse foreman."

She paused, and her cheeks turned pink. "But of course, I left out one qualification," she added. "You had to have the mentality of a crook."

"Another odd thing about our investigation," Frank observed, "was that the gang seemed to be a step or two ahead of us all the way along."

Joe turned to Ray and said, "You tried to scare me off the minute I set foot in this place. Why?"

Ray chewed on the corner of his mustache and said, "Linc told me to. He said a couple of snoopers

146

were trying to foul up our operation, and one was going to be working here undercover."

"When did he say that? Before I showed up?" Joe asked.

"That's right," Ray replied. "When I came in that morning."

Joe looked around the room and said, "Not many people had that information to pass on. I did, and so did my brother, Frank. Karla told someone, in Wombat's personnel department."

"One other person knew," Frank said. "Someone who, it so happens, has direct responsibility for sales in this area, but not in the rest of the country. Someone who has a reason to want revenge against the new management of the Wombat Corporation, which is planning to eliminate his department and his job. Someone who knew our plans right from the beginning. Winston Brinkstead, Wombat's vice president for national sales."

Karla turned and stared at her companion. "Win?" she said, a worried expression on her face. "No way. Win, tell them how ridiculous that is. You've been at the company almost since the beginning. You wouldn't try to ruin it."

Brinkstead didn't seem to hear her. After a long silence he cleared his throat, then said, "You can't prove anything against me."

"Maybe not," Frank agreed. "Still—" He looked over his shoulder. "Eric? Do you recognize this man?"

"Mr. Brinkstead? Sure," Eric replied with a nod.

"He's in Benlow's every week or two. He comes by to get orders and collect money."

"What do you mean by 'money'?" Frank probed. "A check?"

Eric laughed. "No, the checks get sent by mail. What he picks up is in cash. Lots of it. I got a peek inside the envelope one time. Mr. Benlow just about had a fit."

Frank turned back to Karla. "Can you think of any reason that a big retailer might give an envelope full of cash to a Wombat executive?"

Karla's face was grim. "Some companies might pass cash to a retailer, to get a better placement in the store," she said. "We never do. We don't have to. But a retailer passing cash to the company? Forget it—no way."

"It makes sense if the retailer is paying for a big shipment of counterfeit shoes," Joe began.

"Wait!" Brinkstead said loudly. His face was pale, and a thin line of perspiration gleamed along his forehead. "This is idiotic! If I'd set up this criminal operation or been part of it, why would I have told you boys to investigate? Why would I have given you all the help I did?"

"You must have realized we were going to stay on the case, with or without your cooperation," Frank replied. "Pretending to help us was a good way to keep tabs on us. Maybe you didn't think we would get anywhere."

Con Riley cut in. "You wouldn't be the first one to underestimate the Hardys."

148

"Wait, I just remembered something," Brinkstead said. "I *did* pick up an envelope from Benlow once. I was at the store and happened to mention to him that I was on my way to the warehouse. He asked if I'd mind taking it to Linc for him. I have no idea what was in it, but——"

Metairie broke free from the grip of the two police officers and lunged at Brinkstead. The hefty man's hands were still in cuffs, but he managed to butt the executive in the stomach with his head before the officers pulled him away from Brinkstead.

"You!" Metairie exclaimed. "You think I'm going to take the fall for you? Not a chance!" He looked around at the circle of listeners. "He's the one who set up the whole operation!" he cried. "He even ordered us not to do too good a job of making the phonies. He *wanted* them to fall apart. He wanted to ruin the company's reputation."

"You idiot!" Brinkstead said. "They didn't have a scrap of evidence against me. They didn't have any case at all!"

"Maybe not," Frank said as Sergeant Prince took a card from her pocket and read Brinkstead his rights. "But now the shoe is on the other foot!"

On Saturday morning Bayport and Holman High took part in a track meet held at Holman Heights. Once they got to the meet, Frank and Joe spotted Eric near the track with the other Holman High team members.

149

Eric noticed the Hardys and came over. He looked down at Joe's running shoes and said, "You're still wearing Wombats, after everything that happened?"

Joe smiled. "They were a present from the company," he said. "I *know* these are genuine."

"One thing I've been wondering about," Eric continued. "What made you guys think I might be part of that scam? The fact that I worked at Benlow's?"

"Partly," Frank replied. "But we also saw you driving your brother's black four-by-four. One of the crooks had a four-by-four that looked a lot like it. It took us a while to straighten out the confusion."

"That brother of mine," Eric said, shaking his head. "He's nothing but trouble for me! To think that I ran away from you that night you came to the house, just so I could warn him about you two."

"I hope your brother realizes he's making a mistake harassing Devin," Frank said.

Eric shrugged. "I think he does. This whole thing has made him realize a lot."

A voice announced through the loudspeaker that the hundred-meter dash was about to start. Joe and Eric exchanged a glance, then hurried away.

"Go for it!" Frank called out as they left. He strolled over to watch the finish, hoping there wouldn't be any more exploding track shoes. The race was practically a repetition of the one the week before. Once again Eric and Joe managed to pull

150

ahead of the pack. As they passed the spot where Frank was watching, it looked as if Joe might be slightly in the lead. But at the finish line Eric was in first place, by mere seconds.

Frank went over to congratulate Joe on taking second place. Then both Hardys walked to where Eric was standing, catching his breath.

"Congratulations," Joe said, shaking Eric's hand.

"Thanks," Eric said. "You really had me worried today. But you know what? I think I would have beat you in the hundred-meter last week, even if that shoe hadn't popped on you."

"Oh, yeah?" Joe said, glancing sideways at Eric.

Then he grinned as Eric clapped him on the shoulder and added, "But when it comes to solving crimes, you and your brother can give anybody a run for his money!"

THE HARDY BOYS® SERIES By Franklin W. Dixon

☐ #59: NIGHT OF THE WEREWOLF	70993-3/$3.50	
☐ #60: MYSTERY OF THE SAMURAI		
SWORD	67302-5/$3.99	
☐ #61: THE PENTAGON SPY	67221-5/$3.99	
☐ #62: THE APEMAN'S SECRET	69068-X/$3.50	
☐ #63: THE MUMMY CASE	64289-9/$3.99	
☐ #64: MYSTERY OF SMUGGLERS COVE	66229-5/$3.50	
☐ #65: THE STONE IDOL	69402-2/$3.50	
☐ #66: THE VANISHING THIEVES	63890-4/$3.99	
☐ #67: THE OUTLAW'S SILVER	74229-9/$3.50	
☐ #68: DEADLY CHASE	62477-6/$3.50	
☐ #69: THE FOUR-HEADED DRAGON	65797-6/$3.50	
☐ #70: THE INFINITY CLUE	69154-6/$3.50	
☐ #71: TRACK OF THE ZOMBIE	62623-X/$3.50	
☐ #72: THE VOODOO PLOT	64287-1/$3.99	
☐ #73: THE BILLION DOLLAR		
RANSOM	66228-7/$3.50	
☐ #74: TIC-TAC TERROR	66858-7/$3.50	
☐ #75: TRAPPED AT SEA	64290-1/$3.50	
☐ #76: GAME PLAN FOR DISASTER	72321-9/$3.50	
☐ #77: THE CRIMSON FLAME	64286-3/$3.99	
☐ #78: CAVE IN	69486-3/$3.50	
☐ #79: SKY SABOTAGE	62625-6/$3.50	
☐ #80: THE ROARING RIVER		
MYSTERY	73004-5/$3.50	
☐ #81: THE DEMON'S DEN	62622-1/$3.50	
☐ #82: THE BLACKWING PUZZLE	70472-9/$3.50	
☐ #83: THE SWAMP MONSTER	49727-8/$3.50	
☐ #84: REVENGE OF THE DESERT		
PHANTOM	49729-4/$3.50	
☐ #85: SKYFIRE PUZZLE	67458-7/$3.50	
☐ #86: THE MYSTERY OF THE		
SILVER STAR	64374-6/$3.50	
☐ #87: PROGRAM FOR DESTRUCTION	64895-0/$3.99	
☐ #88: TRICKY BUSINESS	64973-6/$3.99	
☐ #89: THE SKY BLUE FRAME	64974-4/$3.50	
☐ #90: DANGER ON THE DIAMOND	63425-9/$3.99	

☐ #91: SHIELD OF FEAR	66308-9/$3.50	
☐ #92: THE SHADOW KILLERS	66309-7/$3.99	
☐ #93: THE SEPENT'S TOOTH		
MYSTERY	66310-0/$3.50	
☐ #94: BREAKDOWN IN AXEBLADE	66311-9/$3.50	
☐ #95: DANGER ON THE AIR	66305-4/$3.50	
☐ #96: WIPEOUT	66306-2/$3.50	
☐ #97: CAST OF CRIMINALS	66307-0/$3.50	
☐ #98: SPARK OF SUSPICION	66304-6/$3.99	
☐ #99: DUNGEON OF DOOM	69449-9/$3.50	
☐ #100: THE SECRET OF ISLAND		
TREASURE	69450-2/$3.50	
☐ #101: THE MONEY HUNT	69451-0/$3.50	
☐ #102: TERMINAL SHOCK	69288-7/$3.50	
☐ #103: THE MILLION-DOLLAR		
NIGHTMARE	69272-0/$3.99	
☐ #104: TRICKS OF THE TRADE	69273-9/$3.50	
☐ #105: THE SMOKE SCREEN		
MYSTERY	69274-7/$3.99	
☐ #106: ATTACK OF THE		
VIDEO VILLIANS	69275-5/$3.99	
☐ #107: PANIC ON GULL ISLAND	69276-3/$3.99	
☐ #108: FEAR ON WHEELS	69277-1/$3.99	
☐ #109: THE PRIME-TIME CRIME	69278-X/$3.50	
☐ #110: THE SECRET OF SIGMA SEVEN	72717-6/$3.99	
☐ #111: THREE-RING TERROR	73057-6/$3.99	
☐ #112: THE DEMOLITION MISSION	73058-4/$3.99	
☐ #113: RADICAL MOVES	73060-6/$3.99	
☐ #114: THE CASE OF THE		
COUNTERFEIT CRIMINALS	73061-4/$3.99	
☐ #115: SABOTAGE AT SPORTS CITY	73062-2/$3.99	
☐ #116: ROCK 'N' ROLL RENEGADES	73063-0/$3.99	
☐ #117: THE BASEBALL CARD CONSPIRACY	73064-9/$3.99	
☐ #118: DANGER IN THE FOURTH DIMENSION	79308-X/$3.99	
☐ #119: TROUBLE AT COYOTE CANYON	79309-8/$3.99	
☐ #120: CASE OF THE COSMIC KIDNAPPING	79310-1/$3.99	
☐ THE HARDY BOYS GHOST STORIES	69133-3/$3.50	